WHERE THE LIGHT NO LONGER FOLLOWS

a love story

WENDY HEISS

BLUE FAIRYTALE NOVELS

To everyone whose mind is like a sea that has tried to drown them.

Content warnings

Suicide, death, mention of rape, mention of abuse and assault.

This book contains explicit content (sex on page), only suitable for adults (+18).

Foreword

These novellas are considered love stories, they are not categorised as romance or *romantasy* or fantasy romance even though there are elements of both fantasy and romance (the closest category it can be placed is *literary romance* with elements of fantasy). I feel that I have to specify that they are not plot heavy, nor is the plot a main focus. These are just a few short stories focusing on two people in love, with characterization as a main focus. The intention for the story was to be fast paced, sweet, and short.

Contents

One o' Clock

Out of all the worlds Silene had visited, she hated this one the most. Tall, towering buildings surrounded her, and noise of all kinds blared around her, none made from nature itself. Cars, mobile phones, planes, and construction sites. A wild nightmare. Even the air was unnatural, tainted with smoke and dust, tainted with gloom and rushing footsteps.

Grey—if there was a colour to describe Asador, it was that. Even Asphodel, the Death God's realm, was more colourful. But then Silene had always found more colour in dying than living. She might be too partial to compare.

Her presence slipped unnoticed as she weaved between the throng of people rushing towards something that Silene couldn't comprehend to be so important that they were tripping over one another, shouting at one another, shoving at one another in order to reach it. Even though humans couldn't see her, they all shivered as she made her way between them towards what looked like an anomaly amongst the rest—a small stone temple or chapel hidden between two tall buildings made entirely of glass. Silene never kept track of what Gods or deities humans prayed to, or what shrines they built to adore them. It didn't matter in the end. They all ended up in Death's hands. Though Azriel was a kind God, she didn't think there were enough chapels or temples humans could build to have him spare a prayer for them. Death spared nothing. Everything had an expiration date as long as he exited. And Silene was there to collect for him. But for some reason, she couldn't make herself step past the entrance towards where a young couple stood holding hands before a priest. A bride and a groom. A wedding.

The hairs at the back of her neck rose when a strange chill swept inside the chapel, gooseflesh spreading down her arms—arms that were no longer capable of any feeling at all. Silene was merely a presence. An augur. Half a soul made up entirely of death, the very essence of dying. One made a Reaper, a servant of Death, when she'd died a few hundred years ago in a realm almost as miserable as this one. Her touch was perhaps the most lethal out of all to one's soul. She was the most lethal thing to walk amongst the living. But there was just one thing that was lethal to her. Just one. One that had been lethal to her long before she'd died.

There had only been a few instances when her un-feeling body had reacted to anything or entirely at all. And all those moments had one thing in common.

A presence. Somewhat man. Somewhat God.

He looked like all three.

It was how he deceived, hiding behind that tall human figure, taller than most, taller than his brother even, dressed in jeans and a white t-shirt that let you see all of the artwork in his upper body. He always attempted to blend amongst humans. Yet, she wasn't sure if anything human or not had bought it. No one possessing his face would ever be able to blend amongst humans entirely. Nothing about him looked human to Silene.

He leaned against the other side of the chapel's arched doorway, not even five feet away from her. And that was somehow the closest he'd ever gotten to Silene. She could now finally see behind the shade of his soft, blonde curls that fell over his brow, shielding his piercing gaze with shadows. From afar, she'd always thought his eyes to be dark, just like his brother's, but they were such a strange shade of blue. Like an ocean being touched by thunder, bright speckles of lightning scattered here and there between the torpid foamy waves.

Silene had seen him many times before, always across the gates of Asphodel, the realm that was now her home and her prison until her five-hundred-year servitude to Death would soon end. She'd seen him many times from afar. Spoken to him, too, when she'd been unable to escape the opportunity.

But not once, not ever had he made himself seen whilst she was working. Or so near her.

There was something akin to resentment between them. She knew her reasons for her resentment, but she could not even begin to fathom his.

Even though they knew so little about one another, some silent history had always existed between them. A history both refused to acknowledge. One she was hoping to never acknowledge.

"What's with all the lace? Are you a tablecloth?" he asked, not even looking at her, his voice much harsher and raspier from this new distance between them. There was not an ounce of gentility in his vowels. It made Silene wonder if the distant space between them had hid this truth to protect her or to deceive her.

Still a little taken aback, her gaze darted down to her black, ankle length dress grazing her boots. "It's really pretty. Do you think we all wear a black cloak and carry a scythe around everywhere we go?" Death was just as lonely as life had been for her, but at least she now had the means to give herself nice things, to make and wear pretty things, to smile at herself in the mirrors she passed. She'd always wanted to learn how to crochet, and it was the first thing she'd done when she'd died. She'd crocheted so many things. From clothes to table centre pieces to curtains and more clothes. She'd even knitted Azriel a few shirts he'd reluctantly worn when he went over to drink tea with her some lonely afternoons neither of the two knew how to spend with another but at least had tried to.

He turned to her, those hardened eyes meeting hers, softening as he beheld her, and Silene wondered if this was another trick the space between them was starting to play on her. "Who are you looking pretty for? No one can see you."

For a second, she'd also forgotten what an absolute prick he was. "*You* can see me." And she could see herself, too. That was more than she'd ever begged for when she'd been alive—to not be seen and leered and beheld by the gaze of others. In a sense, death agreed well with her. It had made her invisible. Untouchable. It had made her everything that she had wished to ever be. Somehow, though, to her deepest chagrin, she was still not invisible to *life*. To him. The one she'd wished the most to be invisible to.

His mouth slowly curled into the most sinful smirk Silene had ever been flashed. "So you got all dolled up for me?"

It wasn't the words that so much stunned her, it was the fact that she felt warm at his teasing which made her either angry or flustered—she could not really tell. Something like her had never felt warm, even when she'd been alive. She'd feared this. That the closer the distance between the two was, the closer she'd be to the scarp that plunged her back into humanity.

"Don't be ridiculous," she said, straightening her shoulders and looking away from him, finally remembering why she had avoided him like the plague for the past five hundred years. "What are you even doing here?" One thing she knew about him for certain was the fact that he did not meddle or interfere, not even witness whatever happened to humans or the worlds they lived in. He was merely a creator who got bored with his creations and let them rampage and stomp all over his own work, all over itself.

"This is the realm I've been staying in."

Her head whipped to him, her mouth curling into a cringe. "This one? Out of all the ones there are?"

"Not fond of it?"

"You can say so." She took another glance at him. "Why are you even talking to me?"

"I always talk to you."

Always was a bit far-fetched. "Not this much." A passing greeting, some snide remarks about her clothing or her hair, shameless flirts he passed around to everyone and anyone, sometimes he even threw a dig in relation to her servitude to his brother, *Death*.

"You keep talking back to me, Silene."

Her first mistake. "Ah, you even remember my name. What a day of miracles," she mused, voice dripping full of sarcasm.

"How can I ever forget my brother's favourite loyal servant?"

There it was. She scratched her cheek absently, and muttered under her breath, "Wouldn't say I'm his favourite."

He chuckled, and Silene fought the urge to look at him. From afar it had been such a despicable sound that mocked her, from this close, it had sounded so warm, as if the sun had shone directly on her. "Are you still crushing on him even after so long?"

Her eyes flew wide. "What? N-no," she stuttered, a little flustered that he still remembered her silly infatuations early into her death. Had she really been that obvious even from afar? "Besides, he is waiting for the human girl he met years ago."

That usual grim shade fell back over his eyes again and he turned his attention to the young couple preparing to recite their marital vows. "We can still love things that don't love us back."

Even though Silene did not love Azriel the way he had meant it, she didn't say anything else, forcing her attention on the altar as well. From time to time, she threw quick glances at Gabriel, at his blonde hair that fell in soft curls a little longer than most kept it, the ring piercing on his lip that he was nudging with the tip of his tongue, his eyes that were a little too dull, too empty to belong to the God who had given life to almost everything Silene had once touched, breathed, seen, and felt.

"See something you like?" he asked, startling her.

"Still searching."

His tongue pressed against his cheek as he smiled ahead.

"This realm is the most miserable place to hide in," she found herself commenting, feeling persuaded to break the awkwardness.

He glanced at her. "Hide?"

"You haven't visited Azriel in a long while. Your brother even sent looking for you. If he wasn't able to find you, I can only guess it is because you were hiding."

"Maybe I was." Lifting a finger up, he pressed it to his lips. "Let's keep this a secret."

"I can't lie to him if he asks me. You shouldn't have shown yourself if you didn't want me to tell on you."

"Then how would you see me?"

She blinked once. "Why would I need to see you?"

He raked one long look over her. "Maybe I needed to see you." Pushing from the door arch, he strode to her until they were just two feet apart, and Silene almost found herself recoiling. Not as much afraid of what would happen to something like her if she was grazed by his deadly touch, but because she was afraid of feeling remotely human again. "To keep an eye on you and make sure you do your job properly," he said. "Wouldn't want you screwing things up only five deaths away from finishing your service to Az."

Forcing her feet to obey her command to stay still and not back away like a coward, she asked, "What are you? My keeper? The work bureau?"

"Are they above me?"

"To me? Yes."

He put a hand to his chest where Silene was almost sure there was nothing under. "Your disregard hurts my feelings a little."

This was the closest he'd been to making her smile. Satisfaction filling her. "Then leave so I can do my job properly," she said, pointing at *timekeeper*, the magic touched, silver pocket watch gifted to her by *Time* herself when she'd been made a Reaper. The very same watch that had stopped working all of the sudden. The very same watch that was never meant to stop even when death or life would cease to exist. There was only one person capable of stopping *death's time* from running, and he was standing all so close to her.

He tipped his chin at the couple. "Let them marry. Time wouldn't mind us borrowing just a minute."

"Time might not," Silene said. "But right now they are just two people who love one another. In another minute it will become eternal. He won't die as her lover. He will die as her husband. As her forever. Bound to her by human vows not even Gods will ever understand the meaning to. You could give them one more minute, but you would be taking eternity from her."

He tilted his head back, his eyes curiously boring into hers. "How can you always make me feel like the bad guy?"

Always? That word irked her when he knew how her end had come from his own gilded hands.

Silene had always made sure to keep most of her thoughts about him to herself. Unlike now. "You've never been the good guy, Gabriel."

"How so?" he asked, amusement flashing across his face as he studied her with a gaze filled with some sort of fascination.

She looked at the couple who'd finished their vows and were about to exchange rings. "You always seem to think you're wanted or needed."

Suddenly, Gabriel stepped away from the chapel, and the watch in her hand started ticking again. Time was following its course anew and death was chasing along.

Silene watched the myriad of emotions catapulting around the house of prayer as the woman's lover clutched his heart and drew out a choked breath before dropping to his knees. Screams followed by cries reverberated around the four walls that had been filled with so much laughter not even a minute ago. Even though his heart had been weak since birth, even though he'd lived longer than what Death had originally planned for him to live, Silene couldn't help but feel guilt. That was her curse. It wasn't her lethal presence that had been gifted by Azriel hundreds of years ago when she'd stepped on his lands. Her curse was to feel guilt she didn't deserve to carry. It wasn't her fault. She was merely a messenger. A guide. But she was taking—she was taking something that didn't want to be taken. She'd been cursed to take, just as she'd taken from *him*, the one who was neither man or God and was standing so closely to her.

A moment was all it took for a wedding to turn into a funeral.

The groom's soul watched it all unfold, kneeling beside his *almost* wife who was clutching his cold body to her chest and screaming. He whispered words of love to her, trying to comfort her even in death.

After so long in her duty as a Reaper, Silene knew for certain that if love was all it took to save someone, they'd all be eternal.

When she took slow steps inside the room, the air veiled with death, every shadow pulling and twisting in her direction, regarding her with unwavering attention until she stopped before the groom's soul.

He seemed to know her before she uttered any word. And instead of being questioned about his fate like everyone did in death, or begged to be let go, he instead asked, "Will she be alright?"

To give comfort, you have to know comfort. Silene had never

been good at comforting. "I don't know of life, only of death."

The groom shook his head as he watched his bride, tears welling in his strong eyes. "I can't leave her. Not until I know she is alright." He cried, and Silene's unfeeling heart almost cried, too. "My poor love, how can I leave her?"

Silene's shaking hands curled into fists at her side. "If you stay, you might not be able to ever meet her again in death or any other life. You will linger here for eternity. Aimlessly. Eternally."

His mouth quivered as he tearfully smiled down at his bride. "But I might get to see my unborn son. I might get to see her raise him. I might get to see them together."

"You might."

Tears skittered down his face. "Aren't you supposed to convince me otherwise?"

"We don't stop being human after death. Your will remains. I've never dragged a soul to the afterlife."

"How many of those you were sent to take have stayed behind?"

"None," she truthfully replied. "Because remaining to see and not be able to touch what your heart burns to have is worse than leaving them behind. And I can say that for certain."

"You're like me?"

"I am. But unlike you, I was not fortunate enough to have that choice. My fate has sentenced me to linger, to haunt, to be a ghost of the unkindest nature."

Silene was not used to pity, so it took her aback when he asked with such a gentle, worried voice, "Why?"

"Because I took something I was not supposed to take," she said, closing the *timekeeper* and stepping aside, waiting for the groom to make that decision.

And like she'd expected, the man followed.

Yearning was a disease with a cure. Those strong enough would survive it. They'd conquer it.

Once she made sure the groom's spirit sat on the boat that would sail through the River of Lethe that ran through many worlds to Asphodel, she looked over her shoulder at where Gabriel had leaned against a wall, watching her. "You're still here."

He hummed. "Fascinating work."

She threw a glance around Asador. "Can't say the same. It

is such an unfortunate affair when you hand a paint brush to someone who has no clue how to handle art."

"An artist's job is to create, Silene. How their creation ages and dies is in the hands of the beholders. But you," he started, and Silene braced herself for what was to come, "so strangely, you I have no memory of ever creating or of the beholding hands I put you in. I only know of you...in death."

Maybe because it had been the only significant thing in her vapid life. "I wasn't a memorable existence," was all she said. Silene was sure that the only piece of memory she might have left behind registering her existence was an obituary. It might as well be all. Her body had started rotting before she'd died. She'd already been a corpse before the night she'd died, and the house she had lived in had always been her grave. It was since then she knew men were not beyond desecrating graves, that they were not even trusted with the dead. For in their hands, she'd always been a corpse, and they still had violated her.

His eyes paced between hers. "Impossible. I would have remembered you."

Silene did not know which *God* or *Fate* she owed her thanks to for having shielded her violent life from his eyes. "Why are you so curious out of the sudden?"

"I was there that day," he said, stopping for a moment to look at her before he added, "when you arrived at my brother's gates."

"I saw you as well," she admitted. "Across the river." He'd been the last thing she thought she'd see in death. So close to her. Watching her. Silene could have sworn that when he'd taken that one short step towards her, he would have reached to grab her. But something had stopped him. Something had made him step away, and from then on, he'd never stepped closer ever again.

His head tilted back, regarding her so strangely. "You swayed a little on your feet when you saw my handsome face."

Her jaw twitched. "It was you who swayed."

His grin was wide. "What can I say? I like sad, pretty girls who look at me like they wish nothing more but to bury my existence six feet under."

"You really must be bored."

"Unbearably."

Silene finally looked up at him, doubting her ears that had never heard such melancholy bleed from the voice of the man who beheld everything. "And do I entertain you?"

He shrugged a wide shoulder. "Grab a couple plastic balls and give it a try."

A chuckle escaped her, the most unadulterated thing she'd allowed herself to do in front of someone she loathed more than anything, and she regretted that moment of weakness almost immediately.

Without a word, she turned and headed her way down the street to find another boat that would take her back to Asphodel.

"Why are you always in such a rush?" he asked, appearing right in front of her. "Scared you might actually have some fun or enjoy yourself for once?"

"If you say so," she answered, pocketing her watch.

He reappeared ahead again. "You're always so vague, Silene. Always so mild and plain. So boring."

Silene simply raised a middle finger at the irritating God.

And he only grinned back at her.

Before she turned to leave, she mustered the energy to utter a few more words, "Your brother misses you."

"Aw, isn't that cute? My baby brother misses me."

As she rolled her eyes and made to go on her merry way, something else forced Silene's step falter and turn to him again. "So you came only because you wanted me to give the couple a few more minutes?"

"Unsure if I am being accused or not."

Her eyes narrowed on him. "Why this one?"

"Why not this one?"

"Because you're a selfish bastard."

His smirk turned serpentine. "Your honesty charms me."

She fashioned a bow at him and then turned on her heeled boots towards the invisible river flowing over the busy streets filled with cars honking angrily at the traffic, so clueless how close they stood to the afterlife. That the gates to beyond were so paper-thin.

Just before she reached the boat that usually sailed her back and forth the worlds, she stopped on her tracks, glaring at the presence that was haunting her worse than a Reaper usually haunted spirits.

"This has been the most unpleasant encounter in my many years, as always. Let's not cross paths again."

"Liar!" he shouted back.

And as Gabriel stood there, watching the pretty Reaper vanish into the fog of the invisible river that would carry her back into his brother's lands, a grin stretched across his face. "Silene, Silene," he murmured, testing the forbidding syllables on his tongue—a name he'd not allowed himself to call upon until this very day. Each and every vowel and consonant belonging to that name seemed new to him even though he was probably the one who knew her the longest out of every single creature that had ever existed.

Two o' Clock

ASPHODEL WAS LIKE ANY other realm, maybe even prettier than most realms she'd visited. Except that light was not exactly light, the wind was truly not wind, but night somehow remained the same—filled with haunting dreams.

One thing about being dead that had not changed for Silene was the nightmares. Except that when she woke up now, there was no one there to let her know the nightmare was gone, that it wouldn't chase her, that it was not real. But he was gone, and she'd never find that comfort again.

There was only one person in her life she had truly loved, and she had loved him to her death. His, too. She couldn't have left her brother behind, alone, afraid, in pain. So she had tried to take him with her, only to fail, for there was no fairness in death either, and her love had turned into a curse. A curse she had lived through the past five hundred years for she had taken what was not hers to take—two lives.

So Silene had lived accepting that her nightmares were never gone, that they were chasing her, that they were real.

Silene's mind was like the ocean. There was never an ending

where she'd go into the ocean and the ocean wouldn't drown her. But Silene had always managed to find a way to stay afloat, even when she'd been alive and the ocean had not been an ocean, but a deep abyss where many real monsters lived. Monsters she'd never been able to slay, whose filthy, soot-covered hands she still felt on her unfeeling corpse of a body she now lived in.

She'd found a way to float in the ocean, sometimes by baking food that she could no longer eat, mostly by sowing and knitting the pretty clothes she wore, often even planting pretty flowers in the garden of the home Azriel had gifted her long ago, a small cottage sitting on a lone hill surrounded by an empty horizon of fields planted with daisies and overlooking Lethe.

Silene often allowed herself to wonder. She wondered if the ocean would let her float like this for long, or if it would cease to be merciful to her one day despite the branches she'd been hanging on. The only comfort to the thought was that soon, Silene would no longer wonder. After she would collect four more deaths, she'd be set free. A freedom she didn't really know if she wanted, but one gifted by Death, nonetheless. It would be her price for her service to him. A price that many spent on a new life, a new beginning clean of memories of any past life, a fresh start.

But Silene wanted to vanish. She wanted her being to be erased from existence. She longed to feel herself disappear, to suspend into nothingness, to be so light from memories and existence itself that time would carry her so easily afloat into someplace where she was between nowhere and nothing. A wish she was not sure he'd grant her as the balance of souls would tip against her favour. A wish with a cost she was sure she would not be able to pay for she had nothing to give but riches made of wretched memories.

The small garden metal gate creaked open, but she did not stop ploughing the spot where she would plant her white lilies, the only flowers that did not die from her cold touch that was now a mark of death, the same hands she had used to mark her own death. There was only one who'd ever visited her, only one who had ever stepped inside the place she called home.

Every spirit and entity allowed into Asphodel knew nothing of Silene but of this one thing:

She could not stand to be touched or looked at or spoken to

because none of those had ever been a choice for her before death. Her body and her mind had never quite been her own, not after her father had figured a way to use both to bring him money to spend on liquor he'd later use to wallow for the misfortune that had befallen him for having to resort to selling his own child. Somehow, he'd always been the one who'd needed comforting after the coin he'd received from the men who had violated her body in ways she had never known a body could ever be violated until she'd been in their hands. And Silene, having all the love one could bear, had let him take that comfort. Sometimes almost letting him beat her to death, sometimes by letting whoever would pay him to beat her almost to death. But dying meant leaving her brother behind, so against every single desire of hers, she'd resisted death. For him, for her brother Luke. Because if she had died, it meant her fate would be passed to him. It was the only inheritance and legacy Silene could leave behind. That rotten fate. For his sake, she'd held on. Until one long night of pain when she'd been barely able to crawl with a pair of broken limbs, bloodied eyes, and an entirely shattered soul.

A shadow fell over her, and she tipped her head back, pulling her garden hat off to look at Death much less welcomingly than when she'd looked at him the night she had died. She frowned up at her oldest friend who never once had frowned back at her despite the fact that he frowned at almost everything else. "You're stealing light from my flowers."

He thrust his hands in his pockets, regarding her with somewhat of a strange look—the look he'd started giving her once she'd reminded him how near she was to fulfilling her duty. "The light in question belongs to me. How is that stealing?"

She rolled her eyes. "What do you want?"

"I have another death for you to collect."

Panic embraced her in a suffocating hug. "It's my day off." She'd never quite imagined time would pass so fast. Silene had so much to do before she'd leave. Her garden was not finished, she'd only re-done half the window curtains for the upstairs floor, and her kitchen needed a second coat of paint because a few dozen years had passed since she'd done it last.

Azriel chuckled. "You don't have days off."

"I request one."

"Request denied."

"These are unfair working hours."

"Complaining is welcome."

"I want to complain."

"Complaint received," he said. "Get your *timekeeper* and head to Asador."

"There again?" Her eyes were already sore from last time. Cement and glass were the last thing she wanted to see at the moment.

"People die every day, Silene," he said with a flare of dramatics so unlike him.

"So not funny," she muttered between her teeth, sneering at him. "Why me? You have about a thousand other Reapers. Why torture me?"

"Because this death is being held hostage, and you seem to be the only one my brother can't get through to."

Silene had no pulse, but something raced against her veins. She swallowed. "Well, if you didn't want him to get through things, you could send a wall."

"He can go through walls."

Her eyes narrowed on him. "Why is he interfering?"

Death stared at her with such a pale regard, never quite allowing himself to make his pity seen because he knew Silene was too proud to accept it kindly. Just like Gabriel had told her, Azriel had strangely not known of her existence either, not until he'd been there to welcome her into his world, where she'd found him watching her life over the reflection of Lethe, the clear waters that bore memories of the dead it carried. "I think you already know. I think you've known for a while."

"Because of you," is what Silene knew he had meant to say. He was interfering because of her.

When Silene had taken what was not hers to take, she'd fallen into debt with another unforgiving God. In a way entirely different from the way she was indebted to Azriel. She'd robbed Gabriel. While she could pay back *Death*, there was no way for her to pay back *Life*. Nor did she want to. In her account, he was indebted to her in ways he also could not pay her back.

In her worst moments, *life* had just kept going. And Silene never quite forgave him for that. A grievance he seemed to know about, too. One she did not want him exploring.

"Don't send me there," she said, lowering her pride just this once. "Please."

"He can't hurt you, Silene."

"You know he can." His presence was like a beacon, a fiery hearth. The closer one got to him, the more alive one felt. It defrosted the very air of death around her, it made her feel human again—in the worst ways possible.

"He won't harm you," Azriel assured. "Never. And you know that, too, Silene."

A box. She'd been sent inside a big, dark box with flashing colourful lights that made her almost nauseous. One where they were playing pounding noise they shamelessly called music while jumping up and down to it. That's where the residents of this dull world found most fun. That and at the bottom of a liquor bottle or a small pill which took their minds out of their bodies, and usually their guts, too.

But Silene had lived too little to fully understand, so she took that moment to observe this side of humanity. The world she'd lived in had been very different from Asador, primitive and poor and sickness filled compared to this one, but in a way, its people were the same. Ghosts. Empty shells made of flesh and bones. Unfeeling. Determined to sink their claws into everything innocent and evil at the same time to find how that high of being human felt. Always at the cost of others. Never thinking of their faults. They'd all learnt to justify their evil.

Silene's ears were pounding along the beat of the monstrous music blasting from the speaker devices overhead. Half of her other senses had also been made void from the rapid flashing lights that flickered in all sorts of colours.

The crowd of people all recoiled when she stepped between it, shivering and emptily searching for the presence they had unwillingly encountered and couldn't see, only feel. Silene was like an omen. One you could only summon once, and only when you grazed the precipices of living.

There, at a slightly raised balcony above the dance floor, sat on a big round table filled with glass bottles of alcohol, stood Jenny, the young woman she'd come for tonight, her name already engraved on the stones of Asphodel.

Silene had never really hesitated. She liked to do what she was sent to do fast. But she was hesitating now. Standing frozen under the steps leading to Jenny as she looked up at the God who had his arm thrown over her shoulders, holding her time hostage for reasons Silene couldn't even begin to think of. All of them seemed to revolve around her considering what Azriel had told her.

Gabriel had stilled, too, staring down at her under his lashes, the crystal glass filled with liquor held stuck to his lips. It was then she noticed how his chest had stilled, too, no longer expanding with a breath.

She didn't understand the surprise in his eyes when he'd been the one to summon her there tonight.

He didn't look away from her as she made her way across the dance floor and started climbing the stairs to him. Gabriel raked one too many long looks over her before those hollow eyes of his met hers, clinging to hers like a magnet.

It frustrated her. Not because she couldn't stand it. It was for a different reason entirely. It was like he could see right through her. Through every single thought of hers.

Gabriel was known for having a thing about skeletons and closets. He never left them alone. If anything, he loved digging up every single bone. He loved to piece them like a puzzle and then scatter them again over fire once he was bored. No story about him was kind.

He set the glass down on the table. "Don't you look pretty for me again, Miss Carver."

She almost reeled back at the name she had not carried since her death, a name gifted to her at birth by the man who'd sired her.

Even though he was far from her, she could almost feel his fingers over her skin, skimming down the length of her limbs for another bone to dig out of her flesh.

"Let go of her," Silene said, standing a few feet from them. He knew very well he couldn't interfere with her work. Yet here he was. Interfering again.

Gabriel only stretched back, pulling the woman even closer—the woman who should have been dead minutes ago. "If only you were a little bit more polite. You're polite to everything. From rocks and trees. You even apologise to ants for stepping on them by mistake. Am I so undeserving?"

"Yes," she responded without waiting for another breath.

Jenny looked around and then blinked up at him. "Who are you talking to?"

The odd God leaned in and flashed her a smirk even though his eyes had rolled in Silene's direction. "A pretty Grim Reaper with a strange, strange fetish for lace who looks like she wants nothing but to stab me to death," he whispered to Jenny, making her burst out laughing.

Gabriel liked games. For some reason, he was now wanting to play them with her. But the thing with dying was that it made one unbothered. Even by the most powerful God there was. Very little impressed Silene. Nothing as much as death did. "I have to take her. Her soul is already dead. If it starts rotting before her body does, we both will be in trouble."

"Then come here," he said. "Come take her."

"You know I can't do that." *Death* and *life* could only meet so close because they never meant to find a middle. It was one or the other, circling the orbits of one another. There were consequences in stepping into one another's space. She'd challenge those rules if not for the fact that she was now merely four deaths away from fulfilling her service.

The smirk he wore told her exactly what she needed to know. He was doing it on purpose. To test her limits or to just simply annoy her, she didn't know, and she wasn't really up to finding out. "I will let you have her if you give me something in exchange."

"Or you can just give me her with nothing in exchange and we can cut this unnecessary interaction."

"I don't particularly want to."

To Silene's much unfortunate luck, she again had no choice when she was faced with life. "Fine. What do you want?"

He smirked as if she was in the possession of some grand power he'd always wanted for himself. "I want so much, Silene," he drawled. "But I don't wish to be greedy, so a day would suffice."

"What day?" she asked, frowning at him.

"One of your days. For a day, you're mine, not my brother's."

Silene swallowed, feeling taken aback at his request. *His?* What had he meant by *his?* "I don't even know if that is possible."

"It is."

"I can't serve you unless he lets me."

He shook his head. "Not serve."

"Then what?"

"Curious, curious, pretty Silene," he cooed. "Patience."

Something was twisting in her numb stomach. "What if he won't let me?"

"He will let you when I ask him."

Her lips parted without words. "Then why did you ask me when you can force me?"

He took a sip from his drink, his eyes still never leaving hers. "Because I'm a gentleman?"

Despite the many words she wanted to throw back at him, the five-hundred-year service Silene had completed under Death's wing was enough to know that any battle started with Gabriel was a lost one.

Life had a penchant for cruelty.

Cruelty only he could deliver.

Cruelty she'd witnessed.

"Fine, have your damn day," Silene blankly said, bringing out her pocket watch and flipping the metallic lid open to count down the seconds till the woman's lifetime would end. "Now hand her to me." The watch was still silent, the pointers frozen ten minutes to twelve as they had been stuck for at least a few hours now. This was how Silene had ended up there tonight.

Pushing from the velvety sofa, he stood and took slow steps in her direction, stopping only an arm's length away from her, the closest he'd ever gotten to her. The space between them always seemed to grow closer and closer each time they'd met. "Tomorrow. Meet me on the rooftop of this building."

"To do what?"

"What does my brother ask you to do besides this?" he said, raking his eyes all over her. "Besides tour guiding."

"Nothing."

"Then we will do nothing," he said, stepping even closer, and Silene held her breath, expecting pain or something else to strike her. "Do I steal your breath away, pretty Silene?"

"Maybe you stink."

He threw his head back and howled with laughter. Silene couldn't help but stare at the column of his throat marked by dark tattoos, she couldn't even stop thinking how it would feel to run her fingers down each of them and through his hair, too. She loved his hair. So soft, always glowing under sunlight, always casting shadows over his eyes to turn the vivid blue into an ocean of tempest.

Life was beautiful.

He'd just not been beautiful to her.

"What are we thinking of now?" he asked, his gaze snaring her. "The things I'd give to know what tortures you're thinking for me."

"I don't think of you."

"Let's not lie."

"Kindly," she added.

"There we are," he cooed, a hint of a smirk ghosting his lips. "Tomorrow, I want to hear every unkind thought you have for me."

"That meeting could be a letter. A very long letter, but I suppose I'd be able to find just enough paper to squeeze in the most important stuff."

"I'm more of a people person." He threw her a wink. "I will see you tomorrow, Silene."

Faster than she could react, the back of his fingers grazed hers as he went past.

She opened her mouth to speak, but he was gone, taking the stairs leisurely.

The spot over her knuckles where he'd touched had turned a

deep purple bruise that felt sore when she raised her other shaking hand to touch the skin that still felt warm from the forbidden contact.

Nothing could hurt Silene.

Nothing but him.

Nothing could ever make Silene feel human again.

Nothing but him.

She could not allow him to get any closer.

"Are you glaring or staring?" he shouted over the deafening music when she remained rooted on the spot, watching him.

"Neither," she shouted back.

"Admiring?"

"Wishing."

"Wishing for what?"

"For you to take a tumble down those stairs," she muttered to herself, and then offered him the sweetest fake smile she could muster when he looked at her over his shoulder.

To her chagrin, he offered her a real one back. "Heard that."

Her lip tipped in a sneer, and she wrenched her attention away from him just as the *timekeeper* on her hand started ticking once again. She sighed, smacking the lid shut and turning to the woman laying lifeless on the sofa. Her spirit stood right above her body, watching herself.

"Hi," Silene started, beginning to recite the same script she had memorised the first day she had been made to serve Death. "My name is Silene. You and I will take a little trip."

"A trip? Trip to where?" Jenny asked, hugging both arms around her unfeeling self. But just like a lost limb, even souls could feel the phantom pains of death a little after they had died. Silene knew it well. For her own phantom pains had lingered a while. Maybe they still did.

"Not far. Not near. A place you've always been close to, but just far enough from."

Gabriel had retired to his home earlier than he had planned to, only so he could watch her.

The penthouse he shared with the grumpiest old man he knew overlooked the river invisible to the human eyes that coincidentally flowed over a busy street between two skyscrapers and disappeared down a square.

Tommy, his cat, scratched the glass wall, unbearably patient as always.

"In a minute, you old idiot," Gabriel muttered. "She will be there in a minute. You know she loves to chat them up first." He chuckled. "Probably telling the girl what a dick I am."

And like he'd predicted, she walked alongside the girl's soul, chatting about with her, the both of them laughing as Silene helped her onto the small boat that would take her to Asphodel.

He watched her wave at the girl's soul as the boat disappeared further down the non-ending river until it entered a body of mist that separated the worlds.

Silene remained rooted there, waiting for another boat for almost half an hour. She did not turn or look or take a walk. Patiently, she waited there, in one spot, hands laced at her front, not moving an inch. As did he. Frozen there at his window, he simply stared at her.

Gabriel bent to pick up his fat cat and brought him to his chest. "Look at her. Isn't she pretty like I've told you?"

Right at that moment, as if she had heard him, Silene turned around to face his building and tipped her head up, forcing Gabriel to hold a breath. She could not see them, that much he was sure about.

He braced himself when she started raising her hand up, nearly folding over from laughter when she gave him a middle finger.

Gabriel wondered—he wondered if she'd always sensed him, if she knew he'd always been watching her for years, for hundreds of them.

Three o' Clock

GABRIEL RARELY MADE HIMSELF seen. Even to the one he loved most—his brother. Ever since they'd been little and new to their existence, they'd been pitted against one another and had been raised to believe that they merely existed as something to stand against each other. Despite never falling for any of it, he'd still been wary of how he loved his brother. Gabriel was afraid—he was afraid to love his brother properly. Truth was, Gabriel was afraid to love anything at all. The only way he'd ever loved had been from afar. As they were now. A river apart and both standing on different sides. He could only love his brother like that without hurting him.

"No," Azriel curtly told him before he could even ask what he'd come there to ask. "The same answer you have gotten from me for the past five hundred years. You're not going anywhere near her. You've already tempted your luck enough by interfering with her work."

Even though his brother's defensiveness towards Silene was not unfounded, a sliver of envy slid into his belly and curled up his gut like a rattle snake full of venom.

Gabriel hated himself for the resentment he'd developed for his brother these past five hundred years. On his guiltless brother who bore none of the faults he'd attributed to him since the day he'd heard of the woman who'd prayed about his own downfall to none other than his own brother out of all.

It was the first time Silene had prayed in her life. A life Gabriel did not know had even existed amongst his realms until that prayer so long ago now—it was how he had found her, amongst the living yet not quite. And that lone prayer had been wasted on his ruination. A plea made to the stars for his damnation. The worst one they could find.

At that time, he'd laughed, revelled in that prayer he'd heard by chance. It had filled him with such unheard amusement. Until he'd chased after it and found its owner. His least regretful mistake, but the one that had cost him the most.

In the end, there had been no prayer to bring him nearly close to the ruin that he was standing in so many feet under. A ruin that he'd sunk into the very moment he'd stayed to watch a human girl with such hate in her heart for him—a hate he'd never seen her possess for anyone else, not even for those who'd hurt her. Before he'd known that the land under him had been quicksand, he'd spent days there on that pale realm, just waiting for her to finally raise her hazel eyes in his direction. Little had he known that the girl had desired the ground more than the skies, and that she would have never looked at him anyway.

"And I've done as you've asked," Gabriel said. "I've stayed away."

Azriel tilted his head, shooting his brother a look full of doubt. "Have you?"

"The best I could." From afar, it had all been from afar.

"You could hurt her. Really hurt her."

Something cracked in his chest at his brother's words. "Never again."

"She is close, Gabe. So close to getting to leave here. So close to a new life."

So close to forever slipping through his fingers, burned out of her memory, burned out of his, too. Once she would fulfil her service to his brother, that's when his punishment would start.

The words burned up his throat like flaming embers dragged by an iron rake as he spoke them, "You think that will keep her away from coming here again as soon as she can? She loved you once. Do you think she will not love you again?"

"Gabriel," his brother warned. "If the fates will have it so, then there is nothing that you nor I can do."

"Is this payback?" Gabriel asked his brother who'd started looking at him with a scornful gaze ever since he'd forced him and his human lover apart years ago.

Azriel shook his head. "Have you always thought so little of me, brother?"

"No."

"Then what is it?"

He didn't know for how much longer he could keep her bones warm before his own would start to grow cold, too. For how much longer he could bear to embrace the soil she'd been buried in that blighted realm he cursed every time he visited because he missed her and was the only way he could hold her without hurting her. "I'm too desperate. Sleeping at her grave every night is not sufficing anymore. Holding the soil her bones lay buried under is not enough anymore. Talking to her gravestone is only making me miss her voice these days. I might be tasting your power, brother. You might have won over me after all. Our father was right."

"Our father is a demented old God." His head lowered and he took off his glasses to rub a hand across his face. "You can only have her for a few hours. The longer she stays away from Asphodel, the more danger she is in. I will intervene if you do anything that puts her in harm's way."

Gabriel nodded. He would have been satisfied even if he'd let him have her for just a minute.

The soft spring wind swept north, and he drew his eyes shut, inhaling the sweet scent of lilies carried with it. If it weren't for the noise below his feet and the sound of humanity buzzing underneath him, he would have thought he was laying on a field somewhere the sun shone hard enough to blind you, not at the edge of a building looking hundred metres below.

She'd always smelled something like summer to him, but when she'd near him, winter would come as shivers spread down the length of his spine like the cold lick of brisk wind.

He smiled up at the darkening skies, feeling her gloomy presence stare onto his back, possibly contemplating every way to his incessant end. "Are you going to stand there all night?" he asked, already drunk in her presence.

Her footsteps were light as she approached him to the ledge of the building where he'd sat. "I was hoping you'd jump and somehow die."

His smile grew into a grin. "You might get your wish."

"To my very unfortunate luck you can't die," she blankly said, taking a seat just a couple feet from him and pulling the black, delicate flower embroidered hood down with an elegance he'd only ever seen her possess. Her fingers had been made only to hold gently, so thin and fragile. He could only begin to imagine how soft the deaths she gave were, how lucky the souls she had touched must have been to be held by those tender fingers.

He looked away from her hands before he'd start to ache for her touch. He could not afford that ache. He was eternal. He didn't think he could live with that hurt for that long. "Maybe not in the human ways you're thinking of. But one can die many other deaths without one's life being taken." As he had often died when he'd seen those tender hands of hers stained with blood while she's held onto life as she'd been beaten and bruised just before his eyes when all he could do was watch.

Gabriel had died his first death then. As he'd stood feet away from her house while she'd knelt down in front of the well, washing that blood off easily as if she'd done it a thousand times. The second death he'd died, his corpse had been buried in her eyes. Eyes that had shone so brightly despite the pain in her body and the open wounds still weeping red while she'd bid her younger brother goodbye with a huge smile as he'd gone to work—a smile that had faded with each step he'd taken away from her. He could recall almost every single one of his deaths. Every single one held her as its gravestone.

She turned to stare at him for a long while, hazel eyes bore into his as if slowly unlocking every single one of his thoughts, peeling back every layer of the secrets he had only ever shared with the wind and his brother, the only ones that had witnessed his breakdown at her feet. "I really hope you've died them all. Every possible death one can die without one's life being taken."

He chuckled despite feeling a sharp spear of ice going straight through his chest. "The stars might hear." Gabriel was not one to seek pity, not hers out of all, he simply did not deserve it, nor would he ever be able to, but he had the unbearable urge to ask that she pities him, that she handles his deaths with those same tender hands. So selfishly, he wanted his corpse to be beheld by that soft touch despite his many crimes.

"I'm hoping they might have already heard me long ago."

As he remained there, unable to look away from her and grappled with fear that he might soon die again, he found himself asking, "Were you afraid of dying?"

But Gabriel knew the truth. He'd watched her long enough to know that she had not been afraid. He'd seen her run in his brother's arms, happy tears clinging to her eyes. But Gabriel had been born with a penchant for pain—he wanted to ache only so he didn't feel like matter, like something only capable of floating. Worst thing was...Gabriel had gotten a taste of it only some time ago, grown fond of the draining, bitter taste of pain, and he'd become addicted, too.

"No," she quietly said, turning to look at the darkening skies that were missing the usual stars unlike other realms. "I was more afraid of living. It is such a burden we are given. Life is such a burden." She sighed as if the weight of a thousand worlds was resting against her chest. "To keep living is a burden when you find no meaning in it, to keep watching years go by as you rot away body and soul with the only thing that could hurt you intact all the way through. If I'd lost my mind, it might have been easier. It would have been a kindness, you know, for you to have granted me that at least."

"You know I can't interfere with human lives, Silene. Many rules forbid me to. As they forbid my brother."

Resting her chin on her shoulder, she looked at him. "I wouldn't have wasted prayers on an arrogant God like you anyway."

"Tell me then, Silene, who did you pray to?"

"No one," she lied to him.

Gabriel's hands curled into fists, forcing himself not to reach for her when her long hair flew up in the air as the wind picked up and tunnelled into a vortex between them. He wanted to comb his fingers through the silky strands for he had such a weakness for her strange hair—white at the front, like the moon, and black at the back like skies of the darkest night. "I will choose to believe that. Only because you lie so prettily."

Her lashes fluttered fast, and she gathered her knees to her chest as if she were cold.

Gabriel shed his leather jacket, closing the distance between them to throw it over her shoulders, careful not to touch her. "I should have asked to meet inside." But he didn't think she'd want to be in a closed space with him or make her uncomfortable. Or worse—afraid.

"It's because of you, you know," she said, looking up at him with such disdain. "That I am cold. I don't get cold. I can't get cold anymore. I haven't been cold in five hundred years." A sigh escaped her as she looked away from him. "I had not realised that I'd missed it." Quickly, she pressed her lips tightly shut, looking like she'd regretted the words she'd spoken.

"Would you like for me to apologise for it?"

"Do you feel sorry?"

He shrugged. "Only that I brought you up here instead of somewhere warmer."

"Why would you care?"

How could he tell her? How could he even begin to explain something so vital to him?

Looking away, he said, "I kept wondering why out of all you've never come to me once in hopes I would grant you another chance at life or a chance at seeing someone you left behind. At some point, the dead always want a bargain with me. Always in death."

He chuckled a little. "They all love me more in death." All except her. Though he'd never found himself seeking to be loved, he didn't want her hate. Not hers. Gabriel had not once kneeled before anything or anyone, king nor queen, God or Goddess, but for whatever he'd done to deserve her hate, he wanted to kneel before her and beg.

"I have never needed a favour," she said.

Another thing he knew but had not wanted to accept. The very few prayers she'd made had been for his demise. And demise had found him. Right at her feet. It had taken him one curious glance at the woman who had made him laugh with her hate, only to find himself not wanting to be hated. "Everyone needs a favour. Everyone needs a favour from me. And I am good at granting them."

"Is that what this is? You want me to ask you for a favour?"

"I just need you to ask me something. Anything. Everyone has questions for me."

"There is nothing I need to know."

"Do you hate me?" The question had slipped faster than he'd intended to ask it. He didn't mean it to seem like an accusation.

Silene's perpetual frown melted away and she turned to look at him again, with something else in her eyes, something like acquiescence, as if she had made peace with the fact that it was neither this or that. "I don't hate you, Gabriel. I just don't like you."

"Why not hate me if I have been so cruel to you?"

"I think I wasn't made capable of hate. All of it might have been easier if I had just found a way to hate. If I had clung to it, I might have found some meaning in living."

"And love? Did you not love?"

"I did. To the point of suffocation. I should have loved a little less, maybe I could have been able to hate more."

He held a burning breath as he asked, "Your death. Was it painful?"

She swallowed, and his eyes dropped to her throat that was always covered by a thin scarf of sorts to hide the scar he might as well have carved with his own hand. "People like me never die violently."

"People like you?" he asked, wanting to know more of the life he'd not been able to witness, of the life she'd always pushed him away from seeing and cursed him to never see. It was like she had not wanted any witnesses to her death. Or maybe...she just had not wanted any visitors at her grave, because the woman he's seen from afar had been neither here nor there, only resembling somewhat of a lovely phantom, a mirage of pain draped in such gentle beauty. She was still as such, same as the day he'd found her and then lost her.

"People who have only ever known violence," she said, standing and handing him his jacket. "I am leaving."

Looking up at her, he said, "You've given my brother your five hundred years. Before you go, give me one more day."

Silene's lips parted, and she stared at him with so much confusion for a while before asking, "Why? At the very least tell me why?"

"I'd like to know more about why you don't like me," he lied.

"Won't take me a whole other day to list them."

"I'm certain you can come up with enough to fill up a whole day."

Her teeth scraped her bottom lip as she thought about it for a moment. "Such a senseless thing to do."

"Says the Reaper who knits and wears things no one can see, cooks what she cannot eat, decorates a house she invites no one into, and plants flowers no one can smell."

Her lips parted and she sat up straight. "How would you know all that?"

"I have senseless hobbies."

"Like watching me?" she asked, blinking fast, her cheeks taking the slightest rosy tint. But strangely, she did not react as surprised as he'd thought.

"That wouldn't be one of them. There is some sense to that."

Her eyes paced between his. "What sense could there even be to watching me?"

He wanted to remember her. Everything about her. He wanted everything about her engraved on his skin, for the ink to take root on his bones, for them to feed into his marrow.

Her entire life was gone somehow except the end. There wasn't a single trace of her anywhere. If not for her hate, he would have never found her, he wouldn't have borne witness of her end, of what drove her to her end.

No one could do that. No one could wish so hard to not exist that their entire existence would erase. But she did, and Gabriel was afraid she would do it again and vanish from his sight once more. Soon, she would leave his sight, and he wanted to use every clue he had to find her no matter where she would hide from him.

She threw his jacket on his lap. "Don't look at me like that."

"Why are you always so unsettled by my attention, Silene?"

"You're an unsettling creature."

He threw his head back and laughed, but that seemed to unsettle her, too, because she looked away, breathing in as if there was no air at all.

"Do I scare you?" he asked, leading her inside.

As they stepped into the lift, she said, "Only what you are."

Gabriel had been adored all of his life. Praised for just his existence alone. Made to feel above all. And finding Silene that one winter night so long ago had been the first time he'd understood his own existence. Without a word, she had taught him so much about himself. For that small period of time when he'd circled her starless, moonless, sunless orbit, he'd found out the truth. Just how feeble and weak he was. How useless he'd been. For all he could do as he'd watched her hurt was to just simply do that—just watch. From afar. Hidden behind shadows of his own faults.

"Why did you bring me here, Gabriel?" she asked as the lift started going down.

His head dropped back on the mirror behind, and he stared at the lift's flickering light. "I didn't want to be alone tonight. Just this one night."

The way her eyes rounded full of understanding he didn't deserve, coloured in with sadness he didn't deserve, might have been his next death—such a gentle one this time. "But why me out of all?"

"Tomorrow," he started, "see me tomorrow, and I will tell you."

Her long silence almost spooked him. He'd almost never felt his heart race before, but it did as she thought about her answer all the way down and as they reached the river. "Does it have to be in the morning?" she asked, hopping on the boat and turning to him. "I wanted to finish planting my new flowers for whoever will stay in my home after I'm gone."

Gone. She'd be gone soon. "It doesn't have to be in the morning."

She sat down, gathered her knees to her chest, and nodded at him as the boat started getting picked up by the current of the invisible river between worlds. "I will come to you since you can't come to me."

He walked along the riverbank beside her boat. "I can come to you, too, Silene."

"But you never cross the river."

He bit down on his smile. "How do you know that I never cross the river?"

Looking away, she said, "You can go now."

"It's a great evening for a walk," he said, keeping the boat's pace. "How do you know I never cross the river?"

She sighed. "I have a great view from my house."

He simply raised a brow. "And do you happen to watch me often?"

"I wouldn't say *often*." Grabbing an oar, she started to row a little faster, making Gabriel's grin grow ear to ear.

The boat came to a stop when he put his foot on the bow and leaned in close to her. "I wonder," he said, watching her chest rise and fall faster and faster the longer he remained there so closely to her. "I wonder how long you have known that I watch you, too."

The ring of hazel thinned the longer her eyes remained on him, her pupils growing wide as if she'd been staring into the sun.

Gabriel hummed at her silence. "Who told you? Az? Some busy body ghost?"

"I felt...saw you," she stuttered. "I saw you."

How had he missed it? How had he missed her attention? "You never said hello."

"I'm not in the business of saluting stalkers."

He raised a brow. "Only murderers and psychopaths?"

"It's my job to guide any soul, regardless. Az deals with them how he wishes to deal with them. I'm not a judge or jury."

"But they get a hello, at least. I don't."

She slowly frowned. "You sound weird."

"My pardon. I only meant to sound envious."

"Will you let go of my boat, please?"

"Sweet dreams, Silene," he whispered near her ear before he pulled back.

Her brows slowly pulled together as he let go of the boat, her expression filled with doubt more than confusion. Her head craned in his direction the whole journey down the river and until she disappeared down the mist.

"Sweet dreams, my ruin," he murmured to the wind.

Four o' Clock

THE MORNING AFTER SHE'D met Gabriel had been strange. She'd woken exactly at sunrise. Not a second after or before. It had been a gentle wake. And Silene never woke up gently. She was always grappled awake by nightmares of the unkindest nature, those made of still memories. Though she could no longer feel tire or rest, she oddly felt rested that morning, full of energy she did not know a creature like her could feel any longer.

But the strangest thing of all?

Silene had seen a meadow. In her dream, she'd been in a meadow, staring directly at the sun. She'd felt herself smile at it, even felt its gentle and kind rays warm her skin.

Then she'd woken up.

Feeling like something was missing and with a strange sensation in her chest that reminded her faintly of longing.

A letter was left on her kitchen table. Only a sentence written in neat handwriting across it.

Did you dream about me?

"No, you creep," she muttered to herself, shaking her head and narrowing her eyes around her house, wondering how he'd managed to get it in her home.

She could have sworn she'd heard his laugh reverberate around her home. A shiver trickled down her spine when new letters started appearing on the paper. *Liar.*

Her lips parted with a silent gasp. "Arrogant creep."

You forgot to add handsome in there.

"Stop it."

You're the one talking to a piece of paper, Silene.

After making sure to tear the letter to tiny little pieces and then feeding all of them to a candle fire, she got her garden clothes on and headed outside.

Silene stood still, unable to move by Lethe, carrying the bucket of water she'd collected from the river for her flowers, holding it tightly to her chest as she looked at where *Death* stood almost every morning and all nights, staring at the bright gates of life across the river, waiting for the human woman who he'd left his heart with to sail through them and back into his arms.

It was a love Silene wanted to envy, but she could never quite allow herself to. Because love had been a fault. Her greatest weakness. She'd loved hard, unconditionally. If anything, Silene had found it hard not to love, for she had been made with a heart so able, a heart that forgave all faults and saw no wrong, a heart that justified those that had hurt it. It was a condition she'd been born with. One without a cure it had seemed.

"How must it feel to be loved by a God," she whispered as a warm gust of wind swept the meadow of daisies—a meadow that had been nothing but charcoal and dust before Azriel had spent seven days on a human realm and had found the love he now couldn't see, nor touch, only wait upon.

"Like a curse," someone answered her. Someone who had a lot of answers for her lately.

With a sigh, she closed her eyes. "You could just let me have this one."

"You are late for our meeting," Gabriel said, grabbing the bucket from her hands and holding it to his side. It was the most ridiculous sight Silene had seen, and she fought the urge to laugh at the most powerful God she knew holding a bucket of water.

She looked down at her *timekeeper* strung on a silver chain around her neck, but it showed her what she expected to see. She was not late—not at all. "You know time rarely exists the way we want it to exist. It doesn't exist at all sometimes even," she said, looking up at *Death* again. "Like when you look at someone you love but cannot yet have."

Gabriel's gaze dropped away from his brother. "I'd hoped you would forget him in time."

Silene couldn't help herself from turning to him, surprise colouring her expression. "Forget who?"

"My brother." A harsh look had fallen over his eyes again. "I understand the fascination with him from afar, but when you get up close he's a real prickly bastard. Not every girl's dream per se."

She snorted, bringing a hand to her mouth to cover her laughter that was turning just a little maniacal at this ridiculous misunderstanding. "I don't love your brother like that, Gabriel. He is my friend, and he reminds me of someone I once knew." She took another glance at the God who had sentenced her to five hundred years of haunting. "Someone I sometimes have wished time would help me forget. But the best time can do is pass. I hope it has passed for him, too. Taken him some place where our memories don't haunt him anymore."

"I can find him for you. You only need to ask me."

She shook her head, heading towards her lone cottage. "I won't haunt him anymore. He needs to be free of the ghost of me. It was all he knew anyway."

Gabriel followed behind her. "Who was he?"

"No one, I suppose. In whatever lifetime he is living, I hope I'm no one to him. Ever again."

Lowering her bucket of water on the small pavement around her garden, he threw a glance up at her cottage. "You live pretty far from the city of Asphodel."

"I've never liked people, and most don't change in death," she said, filling a watering can with some of the river water and spraying it over her lilies. "And I thought you never crossed the river?"

"I do not."

"Yet here you are."

"Yet here I am," he said, filling up another watering can and heading to water the rest of her lilies.

"Why?" she found herself asking, still a little stunned at the fact that the God of Life himself was watering her flowers.

"I thought you wouldn't come."

"I would have come." She'd given him her word.

"Pretty," he said, staring right at her. "Your garden."

Her lashes fluttered fast. "Oh, thank you."

"Lilies."

"The only ones I can touch," she told him. "Oddly, they also used to be my favourite flowers when I was alive. Azriel will not tell me why I can still touch them."

For a second, the corner of his mouth lifted into barely a smile. "Oddly."

Yes, very oddly. "How did you get that letter in my room?"

"If I tell you, I might have to kiss you."

She snorted, nearly laughed, too. Clearing her throat, she asked, "Tea? I keep some for Az when he comes around."

"Does he not have tea in his own damn home? Or is he too busy moping around to make some himself?" he asked, almost sounding bitter.

"I like making tea for him." She gave him a look when he made to speak, and said, "No, it is not because I am madly in love with him."

Still looking like he did not believe her, he followed after her into her home that no one else but Az and her had ever stepped in. It was nothing grand or fascinating, but he took in every single detail with such admiration, studying the paintings on her walls, the trinkets scattered around, running a hand over her sage velvety sofa and the furniture which she'd mostly assembled herself from scratch.

"Black or green tea?" she asked, reaching for the kettle.

"I had another idea," he said, putting a bottle of liquor on her kitchen counter. "I've never had a drinking buddy. My cat is more of a milk kind of guy."

Silene was overtaken by surprise. "You have a cat?"

"He's more of a deity, really, considering he makes me clean his shit and fan him and feed him."

A chuckle sputtered out of her, and she put a hand to her mouth.

His eyes dropped there. "You think I will steal all the babies in the world and sacrifice them for my eternal youth if I see you smile just once?" he asked, uncapping the bottle of the amber-coloured liquor.

Again, she only lifted her middle finger up at him.

"Come here," he beckoned her, sprawling in one of her kitchen chairs, the space around her suddenly seeming so small with him in it, so mundane and pale now that he was there.

Silene's eyes dropped to the clear bottle of golden liquor as she sat beside him. Though she could, she had never touched any human object when she'd entered the living panes. Everything she owed was gifted or given by Azriel, which meant they had lost human value to have ended up in his possession—just like humans, objects had an expiration date. They, too, ended up in graveyards of their own. "I should get glasses."

Before she stood entirely, something pulled at the edge of her thin scarf. "Why make them dirty?" he asked, wrapping a finger around the material and slowly pulling her to sit back down.

Briefly, her gaze rose to his dark one before she reached her trembling fingers to wrap around the bottle neck. The glass was surprisingly cold against her skin. But Silene didn't know she could even tell how things felt. Maybe her skin was cold. Maybe it wasn't the bottle. Maybe she couldn't feel anything at all anymore and everything felt cold to her.

Her fingers came loose, and she pulled her hand back to her side, staring at her palm in fear she'd somehow become human again, or something as feeble and breakable as that, as she had once been.

It was because of him. Life had made her feel like the most fragile thing to have ever been created. And death had made her into an entity worth the fear of many.

Silene reached for it again, counting all of the things she could lose if she felt. The total came to nothing. There wasn't really much to lose anymore.

She felt it. The drink. Even though she wished she hadn't be-cause of the disgusting taste, she felt it. She even felt it burn her throat and then sour her stomach. She could feel it. And when she was done gagging and coughing, she smiled and then giggled like a lunatic, holding the bottle up like it was the greatest invention of Gods and humans both.

Silene's lungs couldn't handle the way she was swallowing air. Like she was mad for it. She was wondering the furthest her mind had taken her in a very long time—she was wondering if she could also bleed.

The realisation struck her so fast that the bottle slipped from her hand. But he caught it before it could splinter on the ground.

"That bad, huh?" he chuckled, pressing the bottle to his mouth and taking one long gulp.

"Disgustingly so," she muttered, coughing.

He pushed the bottle to her again and pointed to the corner of her kitchen. "What's with the cans of paint?"

"I'm redoing the kitchen cabinets. If I have time, I want to paint over the yellow walls. Azriel tells me they are atrocious every chance he gets, and apparently yellow is not a preferred colour to many."

"It's yours. Who cares."

The bottle lowered from her lips, and she rolled her eyes to his. "And how would you know that?"

"Because you have a yellow kitchen. A yellow picket fence. You always wear a yellow raincoat when it rains, and on the wall there is a yellow umbrella with a bunch of bees on it. Your white curtains have yellow daisies on them, your centre pieces are also yellow, there are daffodil paintings all over your living room and around the skirting boards." He took another massive gulp. "Would you like me to continue?"

"No," she muttered, throwing a look around her apparently overly yellow kitchen.

"Why are you redoing it?"

"For whoever will come after me. I want this house to bring them as much comfort as it has brought me."

He simply stared at her, forcing her to look away. "Don't look at me like that."

"Like what?"

"Like you pity me," she said quietly, biting her tongue.

"Maybe I do."

"Well, I pity you, too," she jadedly spat back.

His head angled in her direction. "Why would you pity a God like me?"

Tapping the head of the bottle to his chest, she said, "Because a God like you can be anywhere, do anything, be anyone. Yet, you're here with me. You're really even more pitiful than me."

"You're making some sense," he mused, staring down where she was still pressing the bottle to his chest.

"And you're not. What do you really want with me, Gabriel? You promised to tell me today."

He drank another long gulp. "Companionship?"

"Why mine out of all?"

"I have everything to give and no one to give it to. Use me."

"That does not sound like companionship."

"We can overlook it."

"I don't have friends," she admitted. She only had one friend, Az. And only because he had not let her be and tagged along nearly most days even when she had not wanted company.

"I wouldn't go around shouting that. There isn't a great pride in loneliness."

"Pride is for the living. Besides, you have a brother."

Dropping his head back, he sighed. "As you always seem to remind me."

"You don't have to be alone."

Shaking his head, he chuckled. "Then you know nothing about having a sibling."

"I had one," she admitted. "I had a sibling. A mother and a father. Just like you do." She had it all. In name—only in name. "He was the only friend I've ever needed. My only friend. I think I was his only friend, too, but he used to lie to me so I wouldn't worry about him being alone at work when he left for entire days and sometimes weeks to dig up the mines for whatever little coin they would give him." Silene had never felt the wound she'd thought had closed as raw as she felt it at that moment. And that was the most Silene had spoken of her one life she'd been granted and lived so little, for so little, so lifelessly. Though she had once dreamed of forgetting every agonising moment of that life, she was thankful Death had punished her with the curse of never forgetting a single moment. Silene did not know who she was without pain, and she was afraid—Silene was afraid that if she didn't remember the violence, she would forget who she was. Silene was afraid to live without remembering the pain. She was afraid that she might forgive herself for what she had done.

"You haven't tried to find them?"

She shook her head, taking the bottle and bringing it to her mouth, letting the liquor burn down the ball of longing in her throat. "I'd like to think two out of three are burning in a deep part of Azriel's hell. Over and over."

"And the third?"

"I'd like for him to think I'm burning down there with them."

He took a shaky inhale before asking, "What could you have done for your brother to wish that?"

Silene's throat clogged with a sob. "Does it matter?"

"Of course it matters," he said, heading towards the cans of paint on the corner of her kitchen. "What if you're a murderous psychopath?"

She snorted, her nostrils burning from the liquor she'd had inhaled. "Maybe I am," she said, running a sleeve over her mouth.

"I want to be afraid. If only I could be."

She tried hard not to smile. "You're a murderer's dream victim."

He picked a can of paint and two brushes. "Is your brother the one you wish you were no one to? The one who Azriel reminds you of?"

Her tongue darted to lick her lips, and his attention dropped there. "I don't think I want to tell you. You're not my friend."

"Can we not be friends?"

Silene took one stuttering inhale. "We can't."

"What if we pretend?"

She swallowed. "We can. But it doesn't mean we should."

"We should," he said, standing over her. "We should pretend."

"And what do I get?" she asked, tilting her head up to look at him.

"The lovely experience. Come on, get up. I will help you paint the stupid cabinets."

She blinked fast. "I don't need your help."

"We can do it twice if not thrice as fast, and you're not rich on time to lose doing something this stupid."

Angling a glare at him, she said, "It isn't stupid."

And that is how she'd ended up by his side, painting over her cabinets for almost two hours now. For someone who had never shut up in her presence, he was being oddly quiet. He'd not said a word almost the whole way through the first coat of paint. Nor had she. But they had shared the bottle of liquor between them, silently passing it to the other while they were sat cross legged on the ground and stained all over with paint.

"Why...*beige*?" he suddenly asked.

"It's a well-liked colour."

"It's boring. The sage green was nice. The yellow on the walls is nice, too." He looked at her. "I'm so confused."

"About what?"

"You love colour so much, but why do you never wear it?"

"What makes you think I love it?"

He arched a brow at her. "My mistake. The rainbows behind my back confused me."

Lifting her brush from the bucket, she flicked it in his direction, splattering paint on him. She froze, a hand flying to her mouth, shocked at what she'd done.

Ever so slowly, his head turned in her direction and he wiped the paint from his cheek. "So mature," he said, brushing just the very tip of his paintbrush on her jaw and smearing paint on her face.

Silene's mouth dropped open, and his brush came under her chin, nudging it shut again, smearing more on her skin. "You are inhaling all the paint fumes. Can't be good for you."

"Prick," she hissed under her breath, wiping her face with the back of her sleeve.

He only chuckled, shedding his black leather jacket and throwing it over a chair.

"Colour is for things that are alive," she confessed, carefully painting around a golden cabinet handle, and straining her eyes in an attempt not to glance at the tattoos curling around his thick biceps and down his arms.

"Didn't know colour discriminated like that."

"What's the point?" she muttered under her breath.

"What's the point of anything, Silene? Why does anything have to have a point, or make sense, or have worth, or anything like that? Why can't it just merely exist?" He shook his head, taking a big gulp of the liquor and handing the bottle to her. "Humans are obsessed with putting prices and worth on everything. Valuing and devaluing things that were never meant for them to value or devalue. Anything for the sake of greed, right? Anything for the sake of power. Ingrained in them from the very first breath they take."

"If you loathe humanity so much, why do you help it?" she asked, pressing the bottle to her lips and taking a small sip.

"Because I haven't lost hope in them. They're not all despicable. They're not all deplorable."

She snorted. "Azriel would say the opposite."

"Someone has to still have faith in them."

A long sigh left her lips. "Can't even begin to fathom such a terrible burden," she said quietly.

"There are those who make it nothing but my greatest pleasure." Grabbing a towel, he wiped the paint droppings from his hands. "Let's let that dry. I will come back tomorrow to do the second coat."

"You don't have to do that."

"But I want to," he said, reaching to brush the towel down her jaw and wipe away the paint he'd smeared on her.

Silene waited for a heartbeat, ignoring the gooseflesh starting to spread on her skin. "How did you know about my yellow coat? I must have worn it out like twice, maybe three times."

"It suits you," he told her, reaching closer to wipe under her chin. "You look pretty in yellow."

Azriel materialised in the middle of her kitchen, startling her to her feet. "Get off my realm," he said to his brother, fury painted across his face. "That river is there for a damn reason, Gabe. To not be crossed."

Gabriel dropped the towel and stood, throwing an arm over Azriel's shoulders before smacking a loud kiss on his cheek. "You used to be so much cuter when you were younger."

"And you used to be somewhat saner," his brother said, throwing Gabriel's arm off his shoulder. "Don't know what happened along the way."

"You put a stick up your ass while I politely refused to join your particular kink for woes and misery."

Silene snorted.

"Leave," Azriel told him with finality, throwing Silene a betrayed glance. "You know very well what you'd do to my lands if you remain here long enough."

Gabriel turned to her. "Come with me. There is someone I want you to meet."

She worried her lip between her teeth as she contemplated the offer that she had the strange urge to automatically say yes to. Looking at Azriel, she asked, "Can I go with him?"

He looked the most taken aback she'd ever seen him be. "Why are you asking me?"

"You don't give me days off. What if I get in trouble?"

Azriel rubbed his temple and turned to leave her property, muttering all sorts of things under his breath.

The kettle screamed and roared behind Gabriel as he stood there in the middle of his kitchen, in a house where no one but him and his stupid cat had ever stepped in, his mouth agape as he stared at the most unusual thing he'd ever witnessed in his existence.

Silene was sitting on his couch, stretched over it while she used a scratch toy to pet his twenty-five-year-old cat that was most certainly deathless, eternal, probably even immune to her touch considering he refused to die even at his old age. And when she cooed, murmuring all sorts of praises to the bag of hairy skin and brittle bones by the name of Tommy, he found the irresistible urge to cut that fraction of a memory and play it over and over and over.

His attention returned when she jumped from the couch, walking backwards as Tommy slowly prowled in her direction, meowing and possibly wanting some closer affection. "No, no, no, don't come closer."

"Tommy," Gabriel called, and hauled his archaic cat up to his chest, scratching behind his ears and pressing a kiss to his little pea-brained head. "Silly, old thing. We don't chase pretty girls away. Not how we flirt these days."

"I could have hurt him," she said, her voice low and a little shaken.

"Nah, Tommy is basically immortal." Reaching a hand to her, he said, "Come here."

He hated how she shrunk back into a corner. "I can't take that, and I'm fine standing just here."

His hand lowered back to his side. "Come here, Silene."

Reluctantly, she did as he'd told her, still not coming as close as he'd wanted her to be. "Pet him."

Silene's eyes shot wide. "I cannot. Unless you are offering him as a sacrifice or something strange like that."

Gabriel could not contain his laughter. "Bet I'd not even get candy if I offered his old bones to the God of Abundance himself."

"The cat can hear you," she harshly whispered.

"He's used to me by now."

Her fingers opened and closed into a tight fist at her side before she slowly raised her hand and rested it just above Tommy's head, shaking as it remained midair.

She let out a squeal when Gabriel lifted Tommy up to her hand. "There. See. Immortal cat."

"How?" she asked, trying to bite down her smile as she scratched Tommy under his wrinkly and hairy neck.

"You know how many times this little pile of old bones has been touched by death before I forced him to become a house cat?" When she gave him a sneer, he added, "I keep him alive."

Her hand froze and she pulled it to her side. "You seem to do that a lot. Keep alive things that don't want to be alive."

"Tommy loves being alive," he said, lifting the animal up to smack a dozen kisses to his fat belly. "Don't you? You're just a little stupid."

"What will you do when his time comes?"

"Nothing. Nor he or I have control over that. If it is his time to go, no one can stop it. Unless he runs under a car. That we can definitely stop."

Her teeth sank into her bottom lip. "Isn't that changing fate?"

"There are so many paths to fate. We make choices every day that lead us to many new paths. They erase and form, erase and form all over with every choice we make. If Tommy were to run under a car, would you want me to save him?"

Her lips parted. "Yes. If Tommy wishes to be saved."

Gabriel took a deep breath and let out a sigh. "You're asking me to let go of something I love just because they wish to be let go."

"It isn't for you to choose."

"How is it not? If they let me love them, why won't they let me save them?"

Her gaze shivered as it bore into his. "And if they don't want to be saved?"

"How would they know they don't want to be saved if they've never been saved before? I'd rather take my chances," he said, lowering Tommy on the sofa as he went to grab the teacups. "I'd rather they hate me. I'd rather they blame me and hit me and curse at me than continue to exist knowing I could have done something and didn't."

"I think I want to go back now," she said when he put a teacup on the table for her.

"It's just tea, Silene. Just have a cup of tea with me."

Slowly and very reluctantly, she sat at his dinner table. "Why did you bring me here?"

"Just once," he admitted. "I've wanted to do this just once."

"Do what?"

"Invite someone to my home. Make them a cup of tea. Let them meet Tommy."

Though she did sit down on the other side of the table from him, so close to him, she'd now put up a thousand new walls between them. Gabriel wished he'd never spoken. That he'd just kept quiet to keep her close.

"So, it's just you and Tommy?" she asked, studying the open plane space of his penthouse.

"I've got another room if you'd like to move in. It's mine, but we can share."

Her hazel eyes rolled to him, and for the first time, there was some amusement there along the perpetual resentment for the silent crimes he'd committed to her, the many crimes he was certain she did not even know he'd committed. "How many other women have you offered to lodge here with you?"

"One. Her name was Grace." He pointed his head in Tommy's direction. "His girlfriend. She has been living in my brother's land for four years now. We've not had a girl here since then, that's why he got all excited."

Silene pressed her knuckles to her mouth to hide her smile away from him again. "Your tea making skills suck by the way. I might have been dead for a while, but this is the worst tea I've tasted."

He blinked at her and then down at both their teas. "How can anyone fail at making tea?"

"Did you pour milk before or after you poured the hot water?"

"Before."

Her mouth parted wide. "Blasphemy."

He frowned. "The hot water burns the leaves, and it makes it taste bitter."

"It certainly does not," she said, laughing, not hiding it from him this time.

He wondered if it had been by mistake. "Next time, you make it."

She worried her bottom lip between her teeth for a while before she nodded.

And like that, he might have just secured another day with her.

Another day where he would get the chance to finally confess the truth. He had to. It was bound to come out at some point anyway.

Five o' Clock

THOUGH SHE'D BEEN SENT to Asador again to collect another life, she had not seen who she had thought she'd see. The letter he'd left her this morning had made her think otherwise. Two simple sentences had been written on it: *Wear your yellow coat and take an umbrella. It will be raining today.*

It truly had been raining, and the tiniest part of her was thankful for the warning. There was nothing she hated more than being drenched by rain. Sure, she had felt silly showing up wearing a yellow raincoat to guide a soul to Asphodel, but it had made them laugh.

Just when the weather cleared and Silene thought she might stay and take a peaceful stroll through this pale realm perhaps for the last time, she spun around and pointed her umbrella at him. "You're terrible at this thing." The more she thought about it, the more she realised he'd never really been discreet all the times he'd followed and watched her over the years.

His laughter made her flinch for reasons nothing sane would consider fearful. And of course he noticed, his smile falling entirely. "Really adorable."

"What is?"

"Your umbrella, of course."

Of course. Straightening her shoulders, she returned to her planned walk, determined to ignore him. "Remind me again why am I being stalked?" she shouted over her shoulder, slowing her steps despite the old urges to remain away from him whispering in her ear all sorts of cautionary words.

He appeared right in front of her, blonde hair wet and dripping, and she came to a halt, her eyes wide from nearly crashing into the space that usually always stood between them like an isthmus separating two seas. "There is a show being played tonight just across the street. Accompany me."

A play? "As in *please* or?" she asked, lifting her umbrella between them and pressing the end of it to his chest when he got closer and pushed her raincoat hood down.

"As in you might enjoy it. Could be the last time you can sneak in without paying, or getting noticed," he said, his tumultuous eyes dropping to the umbrella between them. "Or being watched."

"All this comes from the goodness of your heart?"

"So, you *do* think I have one?"

"Well, it still takes a heart to be evil. You'd be less so without one."

"I will keep that in mind," he said, slowly pushing the umbrella down, and leaning in to add, "Maybe I will rip it out and give it to you."

"Why would I want your heart?" she asked, putting the end of her umbrella on his chest again.

"To eat it out." A serpentine smile rose on his face that Silene did not possess enough words to describe how seraphic it looked even under the shadowed light cast from the streetlamps overhead. "You've always looked at me like you wanted to take a bite out of it."

Despite the chill slowly spreading down her limbs, she remained rooted there, out of words, her umbrella lowering. "What play?"

He didn't answer her, and simply started backing away and crossing the street towards an older building hidden between towering glass ones. Forcing her feet to move, she'd followed after him, her eyes latching on his broad back, the distance between them taunting her.

"Stop glaring at me," he said, his voice filled with so much amusement.

"You have a perfect back," she said with an unusual skip in her words, "to stick a knife in it."

"Don't flirt with me, Silene."

In turn, she glared even harder.

"Silene," he warned, and she jolted straight, quickening her steps and jumping over the puddles of water to follow him. "What about tickets?" she asked as they crossed the lobby towards the theatre rooms.

Throwing her a look over his shoulder, he said, "You know what I am, Silene."

She batted her lashes at him, shedding her raincoat. "A rude, arrogant prick?"

"Besides that."

"We can literally be here all day."

He chuckled, grabbing a door handle and pushing it open, pointing for her to go in. Just when she was about to enter, he put a hand on the other side of the door frame, right in front of her face, and leaned in to whisper in her ear, "Do you just follow anyone anywhere they ask you to follow them to?"

"Not particularly."

His eyes dropped all over her face, observing every part of it. "What if I meant harm?"

"What worse can you do to me that you haven't already done?" she asked.

Still, he didn't move from there, their faces merely inches apart. "Tommy says he misses you, and that you should visit again."

Despite the few cold rain drops clinging to her body and the chilly tunnelling breeze in the corridors, Silene felt entirely too warm. "Tommy is such a gentleman. You ought to learn some stuff from him."

"Take that back or it will not be a very good life for Tommy starting now. I will buy him the cheapest kibble and throw out all his toys."

Her tongue pressed against her cheek as she tried really hard not to laugh. "I think you would not do that to the one thing that finds you bearable."

Sarcasm dripped off his tongue when he gave her a smirk and said, "You think too highly of me."

"I assure you, I do not think highly of you at all."

"So, you *do* think about me?" he asked, flashing her a full row of teeth.

"Often," she admitted, lifting her umbrella and resting the silver tip of it under his chin. "All usually involving some mild form of violence." She winked at him. "Pew."

"What did I tell you about flirting with me?"

She rolled her eyes and ducked under his arm, eyeing the wide space of the theatre with so much relish. She'd never been in one, and they were just as magnificent as the pictures on the human magazines. Silene had rules. Many which she had broken in the very short time of three days she'd been hanging around him. She never stepped in human spaces unless she was there to collect a death.

He pointed to an empty red-velvet seat among the many and then went to sit a seat further from hers when she put her umbrella and raincoat between them, a barrier she felt like it needed to be there to remind her of what he was and what she was, something that was starting to blur in her thoughts—in her actions, too. What in the stars was she even doing with him? In a theatre out of all?

"Are we early?" she asked, going on her toes to take a peek at the rows under them. "There is only me and you here."

"That's because it is mine."

She blinked at him. "Like...the entire theatre?"

"Indeed."

Her eyes widened just slightly. "Why do you own a theatre?"

"There was this girl I've always wanted to bring to a theatre," he confessed to her.

Her voice dripped with sarcasm when she scoffed, and said, "As there always is, I'm sure. But owning an entire theatre is a bit excessive though."

He raked a hand through his wet hair, pushing it back from his face, and chuckled. But the amusement never quite reached his eyes, and Silene was struck with the realisation that nothing quite reached his eyes—she'd come to realise they were a sole entity, one full of sorrows. "She doesn't like being surrounded by people."

A faint, strange empty sensation settled in her stomach as she studied his strangely dour profile that just reminded her of the terrifying power he beheld—of the powerful God she'd seen from afar. "Did she like this grand gesture of yours?"

"I never really brought her."

"How come?" she asked, not resisting the urge to know.

"There was this one bargain I once made. In exchange for what I wanted, I had to give her up. The only way I could have her at all was if she wanted me to have her. I kept waiting for her to call for me, to ask for me, to want me. It was something unrequited in the end."

Silene did not miss the opportunity to laugh a little at his pain as she always did, but for the first time, she felt a sense of unease for doing so. "Who could possibly dare break your heart, Gabriel?"

He would not look at her even though he always looked at her. "She did. Many times. The fault might be mine. I keep offering it to her, but she does not want my heart. Nor to break it, nor to bury it, nor to tear it up to tiny little pieces. She does not want it at all." The muscles in his jaw tightened, and he swallowed. "What am I to do with a heart I cannot use to love her, Silene?"

Her insides squeezed as if they had been pulled into a tight fist, the air turning a little thick, suffocating her lungs that had just started breathing again after hundreds of years.

Silene's attention was dragged away as actors poured on the stage, dancing their way in with spectacular movements, pouring flower petals and glitter in the air as they jumped and waltzed and sang their hearts out. She clapped along, smiling widely and with fascination, utterly enchanted by the spellbinding grandeur of all the costumes and the bejewelled props—she clapped until her arms felt like falling off. But the longer it went on, the more she looked, the louder the music got, the more she noticed the twisted smiles on the actor's faces, what was staining their hands a crimson red, speckled across their colourful clothes, and their skin. Silene's hands pressed together one last time in a meek clap, her smile slowly fading as she noticed the strange, drunken craze spinning around one lone table that she'd not noticed at all being there all this time, where one lone soul stood and sat beside. No costume, no mask or paint or drawings, no glitter or colour, she was dressed in a tattered nightgown, her face vacant. Through the whole first hour of the play she did not move nor blink, just sat there unnoticed—almost unnoticed to Silene's eye as well. It was such an anomaly amongst the stage. It stood out so sorely, so strangely, like a tumour on a healthy heart. It spoiled the entire vibrant play.

Then lights in the theatre suddenly went out entirely, enshrouding them in darkness, and Silene jolted a little, looking around the abyss surrounding her, hoping for even a small glow from under a door or a keyhole.

Darkness did not scare her much, but what rested inside it did. Her father had often used it to his advantage. He'd acted as if the darkness would hide his sins. That if no one could see what was happening to her, it would not count. That her screams and cries would be drowned by the abyss, taken away once light would rise in the morning. That the darkness could hide the blood better, and that it would make her bruised, thin body more desirable to the ones who he was selling it to.

"Gabriel?" she asked, feeling a lick of fear on her spine that had her shaking after so long. There, seeking him, she felt so human again.

"I'm here."

A long breath of relief left her lips when his voice wrapped her back in warmth.

A cracking sound came from the stage ahead, as if a glass or a plate had broken, and she waited, suddenly feeling something like a pulse grow under her skin. But it couldn't be. Silene had no heart. She had no need for it.

A gleam widened from the stage. Candlelight began growing brighter, forming a halo of light around the table it was perched on top of and the girl sat on a lone chair beside it. Her knees were pulled to her chest, her long dark hair falling around her like a blanket while she stared at the candle without blinking. Everyone else was gone but her.

Silene sat up straight when a heavy feeling settled on her chest at the image before her. An image that struck so familiar to her. The table. The chair. The candle. The girl. Her blood-stained night dress.

There were times she'd spent sat just like that, in front of a flickering flame after the horrors that had been committed to her had ended, confessing every one of her secrets to the light in the pitch of night when everything but her nightmares had gone to sleep. That very same light had eventually started speaking back to her, bringing her comfort nothing had ever given her before.

The flame flickered, growing brighter, showering the girl with light and warmth until she stopped shivering.

"Thank you," she offered.

"Maybe I should thank you," the candle spoke, "for summoning me, for lighting me and letting me burn."

So much pity filled her pain stained eyes. "But you will waste, you will melt and smoulder."

"A victorious end for a candle."

The girl managed a smile, and Silene's heart pulsed so painfully when that smile reminded her of her own. One that looked more like a scar than a smile. "I want a victorious end, too."

A single tear beaded in Silene's eye at those words. Familiar words. Words she'd heard before.

"You have to burn first," the candle said. "Such lovely light and warmth you will give. Though no one will deserve it, no one can ever earn it from you. You will shine like a miracle."

"There is no one to light me," the girl sighed. "Nothing and no one at all. If I let my brother, I'm afraid I might burn his hands. If I let my father, he will smother me and use me as he wishes."

A choked sob ripped from Silene's throat, and she put a hand over her mouth to stifle a cry. Her words were just broken syllables when her head slowly turned to Gabriel, and she said, "What is this?"

"A play," he answered, his voice like gravel.

Then the candle flame asked, "Why do you cry?"

And the girl answered, "Because I am an unhappy person."

Silene could almost hear the *timekeeper* in her pocket stop ticking and time slowly freezing over, the air turning an odd colour tinted with a shade of the past—a past where she'd uttered those very same words back to a strange candle that talked. A mirage of sorts she thought her mind had called to soothe her loneliness, her hopelessness.

Her attention whipped in Gabriel's direction, staring at his stony face as he watched the play ahead with a vacant set of eyes that resembled the depths of stormy, blue waters. Silene could almost swear that somewhere in there he was drowning, just as she was. No one would be able to survive the depths of loss his eyes had caved into.

"An odd thing to do," he said without looking at her, "talking to candles. You did that a lot. Night after night. It was the closest you've ever let me get to you."

Memories rushed to flood her mind, and a chill spread down her spine when she recalled the voice that had talked back to her then. The familiarity of it. The warmth.

No.

No.

He couldn't know her most vulnerable moments, when she had laid her heart bare to the only thing that would listen to her. It had been her imagination. The candlelight had been only something her mind had made up out of desperation. It couldn't have been real.

"How?" she asked, her voice breaking.

"You called. And I could finally hear you. After so long, Silene. After so damn long wishing I could."

She felt exposed. Stripped out of her skin. Bones bare in front of the one God she'd wished would never see her desperation for help. For help she could not find the strength to ask because of the spite she'd had for *life* himself.

"I did not call for you," she shakily whispered. She did not know what or who she'd called at those moments. All memories that had been slightly warm had almost vanished from her mind to make space for all the terrifying ones that only kept growing there like a malign tumour. But the call had not been for him. She was sure she had not asked for him. She had asked for salvation. And the only salvation Silene remembered ever dreaming of, had been a kind death.

"My brother cannot hear the living, Silene. Only I can."

"You shouldn't have answered. I didn't want you."

"I know. I knew."

"Was it fun?" she asked, her voice trembling. "Was it fun to hear about how I had bruised by my father's hands? Did you laugh when I told you he'd sell me out to anyone who gave him enough coin for his next fix? Did you enjoy when I confessed about the first time I had to wash away the blood from between my legs after I'd been raped in my childhood bed? The one I never managed to outgrow because he barely fed me enough to wake. Or sometimes not at all, just so he could call it mercy when I would be unconscious and wouldn't feel what they would do to me."

His eyes drew shut and he took one deep breath, a tremble permeating his body. The entire earth shook with him, chairs and curtains rattling, the ceiling and chandeliers breaking and falling to the ground in a million pieces of crystals.

Her arms came around her body when the crashing sounds made her flinch. "Look at me!" she screamed, her throat swelling with a cry when he did look at her—when he looked at her with such anguish, such burning pain as tears slid down his face.

"There hasn't been a moment ever since the first time I found you that I've looked away."

She shook her head. "You hurt me!" she sobbed, finally breaking down in front of him just like she'd avoided doing. "Forcing each damned breath in my lungs. What was the purpose of my existence? Was I there just to suffer?"

Another silver tear slid down his face, and it was her turn to look away.

The both of them sat there in the dark silence. Eventually the earth did stop trembling, too.

Her voice was vacant and hoarse when she asked, "Should you not ask for forgiveness? One would ask for forgiveness, at least."

"I don't want you to forgive me, Silene."

Her lips trembled as she breathed out a long exhale. "I never will."

"Good. That's good."

Silene's hand pressed to her brow, and she shook her head. "Why did that not feel good at all? I've been wanting to tell you that for a long time," she confessed, wiping her eyes. "I wish I could just hit you." Reaching for an empty bottle of water on the seat next to hers, she threw it at him, hitting him in the head.

He blinked at her.

She blinked back at him, her lips pressed tightly together. She held it in for all ten seconds before snorting into her hand and chuckling, her tear-stained laughter growing the longer he just stared at her stunned.

When her body somewhat settled from the uncontrollable tremble, the mix between a laughter and a cry, she asked, "Why were you there when you knew I did not want you?"

"At first, I hoped that if I waited, I might begin to matter more to you. Only for you to matter more to me in the end."

Silene remained frozen at his confession, unable to look away. She had been nothing. A rock had mattered more than her. A rock would have sold for more than her. She. Had. Been. Nothing. "Why?"

"That day I first saw you," he started, and his eyes found hers like a polarised magnet, but drowned in such depths that they looked entirely black. "I learned more about myself through you that day than I'd ever known about myself in centuries of a lifetime. What had I done? How could I have forgotten you? How could I have left you in those hands?"

She wiped away a lone tear. "You said you didn't remember me."

"Fragments is all I have. Fragments that *Fates* gave away to spite me. All I saw was you getting hurt. Then you'd vanish in and out of my sight like some mirage. No matter how many times I would rake through your world, I could not find you. Not unless you would let me in. And those moments were brief, so brief, Silene. They were enough though."

"Enough...for what?"

He looked away, his head lowering. "I would watch you make things out of nothing." A choked laughter sputtered out of him as if he was recalling some fond memory. "Anything, you could make anything out of nothing. You gave more life to things than I ever could. Simply by touching them. You were magnificent. The rarest thing I'd laid my eyes upon," he said, and the very foundations of her mind shuddered. "You and your brother, neither of you had any hope, the both of you were hurting, but somehow, you could give him courage and make him dream. Without them he would have never returned from those mines. It was what kept him alive in there, do you know that? Do you know how much power you had, Silene?"

Her eyes drew shut as she silently sobbed. She missed her little brother. She missed him so much.

"I wanted," he continued, "I wanted to give it back to you. All that you gave. But you would not let me. You would not let your brother either."

Silene knew. At some point, she had not wanted to be saved. She'd seen no point in seeking him, and hating him had been a comfort—a way for her to justify the end she had been planning. "For so long, I'd been searching for someone to blame," Silene finally said, free of the truth. "And you were the perfect one to blame. For everything." Her eyes squeezed shut, and she swallowed that ball of glass shards down her throat until it settled in her stomach, tearing her insides instead. "Sometimes I wonder why I couldn't find it in me to blame my father, why couldn't I try to kill him instead, why did I keep justifying him."

"Because he stole something from you. Something I should have helped you find again."

She opened her eyes and looked at him. "What?"

"Hope."

She shook her head. "I don't think I wanted hope. It just seemed...easier to let him have it. My brother," she said, smiling at the few happy memories of him she still clung to with all her might, refusing to let them be drowned by the rest. "My sweet brother, he was a dreamer. His dreams used to give him broken bones and bruises. I was never as brave as he was. It's why I chose to be a coward in the end."

"You were not a coward, Silene."

"Don't," she choked out. "Do not tell me that what I did was nothing but cowardly."

He simply looked at her, and she'd already heard every word he did not say out loud.

She shook her head. "Don't do that either. Don't give me back my hope. I don't want it."

"I want to give you everything, Silene. Let me give you everything."

"Why?"

"I want to bring you to a theatre full of people and for you not to fear them."

For a moment, Silene remained frozen, letting his words wash over her. She'd never been so scared as when she asked, "Am I the girl?"

"You are."

She walked mindlessly through the dark streets of Asador that were starting to quiet down with the rising violet dawn tainted by smoke and shielded by the towering buildings. His tall shadow followed after her turn after turn, offering her a comfort she could not even comprehend—a comfort he'd been offering her since long ago, without her even realising.

His jacket was again thrown over her cold shoulders, and somewhat of a twisted smile crossed her face at the chilly wind that blew across her face as she skipped over puddles. She had missed feeling the wind, too. Silene had not realised she could miss such a mundane thing. She wondered when she had ever regarded the wind in her past life. If it had meant so much to her before. Why...why was it filling her heart with so much...so much...cravings? She wanted to dance it in, to run her fingers through its chilly strands, to let her hair billow in it, to close her eyes and trust the darkness behind them.

"You can stop following me now," she said into the wind, hoping it would carry her words to the God behind her.

"I want you again. Let me have you another day."

Silene did not like how her heart began racing. Whether it was from fear or excitement, she did not know. She'd been dead for far too long to remember exactly the difference between the two. "Beg," she said, spinning to him. "Get on your knees and beg for it. Maybe I will consider it."

Instead of the anger and refusal she expected to be flashed, the God was struggling to hold back a smile as he took his hands out of his pockets and went down to his knees before her.

Silene's eyes went wide, and she looked around them as if someone would see and condemn her to many lifetimes of punishment for what she'd done, for bringing a God to his knees.

"Any other request, my great misfortune, my beautiful demise?" he asked, no longer holding back his grin. "Or can I have you for another day?"

He'd lost his godly mind. And she'd lost her voice, maybe her mind, too, as she stared astound at the God at her feet who was looking up at her like she'd never been looked at before.

She took a few steps back, putting distance between them again and praying her heart would go silent and cold as it had been for so many years. Silene could not understand if she entirely loathed the way her existence defrosted in his presence. And that terrified her. "Request denied. You can stand now."

His teeth dug onto his bottom lip as he looked up at her. "I quite like it down here. Have come to realise why humans get on their knees to pray. Certain things do look like quite something to behold from down here."

Her chest rose fast with breaths she didn't know she could take, with breaths she shouldn't be able to take in death. Somehow, when she was close to him, she could breathe. She wanted to relish in that sensation until she remembered that in his presence she could hurt, too.

Unable to find any of her words, she decided to turn and leave him there.

"Am I picking you up or are you coming to me tomorrow?" he shouted from behind her.

"Neither," she replied over her shoulder. "This has been exhausting."

"Deny me, my ruination," he called as she stepped into the boat over Lethe. "It makes begging all the more enjoyable."

"Shouldn't you be busy with—I don't know—whatever your

godly self should be doing?" she shouted back.

His words slipped through the veil between worlds as she entered Asphodel, "I want to be busy with you."

She stomped all the way up the hill to her home, muttering all sorts of cautionary reminders to herself, and almost bumping against Azriel who was standing on her doorstep. "W-What are you doing here?" she asked, rubbing her forehead.

"You were late."

"I went to a...uh, to a theatre," she said, inviting him in as she always did, putting the kettle on the stove.

He arched a dark brow and took a seat at her dinner table, not filling the space quite like his brother had. "You went to the theatre. And how was that?"

"He knows me," she said, pulling a teacup and saucer from her shelves. "From before."

"Who does?"

"Gabriel."

"Hm," he hummed, sipping on his tea.

Silene's lips parted. "You knew?"

"How much did he tell you?"

She blinked fast. "How much should he be telling me?"

"None of it. I warned him not to."

She gapped. "Warned him? Why would you warn him?"

"It's for the best of both of you to leave behind what was meant to be left behind."

The tea cup almost slipped from her hands. "You've kept him away from me?"

"Have you wanted him to get close to you?"

Silene might have mulled over that one question many, many, many times over the next few mornings and nights.

Six o' Clock

THAT NIGHT, AS SHE had done many nights ever since she'd found out the truth, she sat at her dressing table, her knees gathered to her chest, staring at candle light flickering for hours to no end, until all the wax had melted into puddles, the wick burned entirely out of existence. Then she'd lit another, and another, just watching the flames flicker until she'd fallen asleep just like that. On the chair, her head resting on top of her knees, while she stared at his letters piling on top of one another on her table.

They started with: *Miss me already?*

The next day he'd written: *You will have to leave your room. Your lilies look like they need water.*

And the next day it read: *I've watered your lilies, you cruel Reaper.*

And the very next: *You must miss me. Surely, you miss me.*

Then again, the very next: *Let me see you. Fine, let Tommy see you.*

And another: *Come out of that damn home and glare at me, shout at me, come out and throw rocks at me, and tell me every single thing you hate about me, but just come out. Please. I can let you throw stuff at Tommy, too, if you'd like. PS: Your lilies are looking a little sad. Are their stems supposed to be bending like that?*

Her eyes started drifting shut, lulled by the flame, a drunken smile etched on her face from the last letter he'd sent her and the glances she'd stolen outside of her garden these past few days of the terrifying God who'd been overwatering her lilies. She did not know if it was the faint candlelight or the exhaust she'd been feeling lately, or if she'd simply gotten drunk on the silly words on the very last letter: *I might have overwatered your lilies. They're looking a little odd.*

"Just go lay in bed already, Silene. You can't keep sleeping like that forever."

Her eyes popped open, and she stared at the flame, leaning in to whisper, "You did not speak, you're a candle."

"No," the same voice said, now from behind her. "But I did."

She almost dropped from her chair when she spun in his direction so fast she got dizzy. Gabriel stepped forward as if to catch her, his hands freezing merely inches away from her body before he pulled back, his fingers curling into tight fists as they returned to his side.

"Why are you here?" she asked, her hand flying to her throat out of instinct, to make sure the scarf was there, hiding her scar—a scar he'd already known about.

"There is something I can't stop thinking about," he said, circling her room and stopping to inspect a bunch of little trinkets she had carved out of wood back when pottery had been a miss. Five hundred years was a long time. One could not have too many hobbies. Or make enough carved figurines, so there were...a lot...everywhere, almost annoyingly like glitter speckles. She was a hoarder. And so what?

"Like what?" she asked, looking down at herself to make sure her pyjamas were not askew while he wasn't paying attention.

"You," he admitted, leaning against her vanity, right there, not even a foot from her. "And it doesn't help that you won't let me see you."

She was hoping to the stars her cold corpse could not blush because she might have...would have. "You can't come into my home like this."

He moved to her window, trailing his fingers down the curtains she'd made, pinching the trimming between his fingers. For some reason, he smiled down at it. "The door was open."

"The door is always open." No one came to her home.

"Maybe you should start closing it," he said, reaching for a vase filled with a bunch of roses she'd made out of copper wire, and grabbing one, studying the detailed work that had gone into shaping the second kind of flower that could never wilt by her touch. "How does everything you touch turn out so perfect? The garden, the home, the clothes, the little paintings on the walls, these," he said, taking a figurine and turning to look at the rest of her room with a strange sort of awe. "Everything on here."

A little flustered laughter left her, and she looked away from him, narrowing her eyes on the mirror and scrutinising the unusual flush on her cheeks. "They're not perfect."

"One day," he started, his voice languid, "I watched you sit on a wood stump just outside your home, holding a pair of trousers nearly shredded and a threaded needle in your other hand. If I had not been so distracted by how happy you looked doing something so menial, I might have been able to find out the secret to how you made them look brand new."

Her insides gripped in a tight fist. "They were my brother's," she said, smiling while hot tears lined her eyes at the memory he'd just invoked. "He'd always tear them up in the mines. I couldn't wait for him to get home to show him how I'd fixed them. He'd call me a witch and haul me around until I'd admit I possessed magic he wasn't aware of."

"Why were you outside that day? You barely left your home, and it was wintertime. Why did you sit in the cold?"

All of the sudden, she felt overtaken by a sense of hollowness. "It was easier to run," she muttered. "He was home—my father. Not drunk enough. Somehow, his worst evil always came when he was sober. The kindest he was to me was always when he was drunk."

The wind blew her windowpanes back so hard the glass shattered against the wall, making her squeal and jump from her seat. The concept of weather did not really exist in Asphodel. There was no such thing as rain or wind or even really sun at all.

Her hand came to her startled chest, and she startled even more when she felt her heart bang against the breastbone. "Please leave now," she begged, starting to back away in her seat. Silene did not want to know what else his presence would cause to her or Asphodel.

"See me in the morning," he said, coming to stand right before her, and she sucked in a stuttering breath as she stared up at his face that was carved out by so many shadows, suddenly so grave and terrifying under them.

"Why should I? Are there any more lies and secrets I should know about?"

"None was a lie or a secret. You've just never asked. You've never even let me get close to you. I can't even count the many ways you've avoided me."

"You're such a frustrating creature."

He smiled, and it melted the ice forming around her again. "Tell me that you will see me tomorrow."

She glanced away from him. "I don't like how you make me feel."

That smile he wore started to slowly fall. "How do I make you feel?"

The most worthless form she had ever been—human. And that was not even the worst part. "Go away, please," she said, turning to the mirror and starting to take the rollers out of her hair. The actual terrifying part was that Silene might have enjoyed it—the very small things she was starting to feel. The things she had never really thought about. Every little reaction her body gave suddenly felt amplified. And she was breathing differently—she was breathing how she'd never breathed before.

"Why won't you talk to me, Silene?"

The way he said her name, how every letter left his lips bewitched the very air she inhaled, almost leaving her heaving. "I hate that I have to look up at you every time I do so," she lied.

He stepped close to her, almost making her drop from her chair again when he got down to his knees right there at her feet. "Now talk to me."

The stars had a wicked sense of humour—so wickedly cruel. How...why were they tempting her like this? Silene didn't wish to trust his intentions, she'd never had trusted his intentions even when she'd been alive. But she was finding it hard not to. Maybe, apart of her wanted to trust them. Maybe just this once. Just this once she wanted to try...to try how it felt—how it felt to be alive. What would go wrong? She was already dead. This was her best bet of ever knowing fully.

Reaching for a small shelf on her vanity, she pulled a piece of paper she had scribbled on, folded, and unfolded about a thousand times, contemplating this very moment.

He raised a brow as he took it and unfolded it, reading its small content with his brows pulled together. "What is this?"

"My demands. For my time."

He lowered his head a little, looking like he was trying to hold back a smile before he asked, "Are you bargaining with me, Silene?"

"No, *you*'re bargaining with me, Gabriel." She stood, now towering over him. "Do you accept them?"

His eyes drew shut and his head dropped forward, not even an inch away from resting against her stomach. "I do," he said, his breath brushing against the very thin sliver between her night shirt and trousers.

Silene felt her limbs weaken, grow as soft as tulip stems, her knees almost buckling at his nearness. "You might wait downstairs while I get dressed. Also, get up now, your knees will leave a mark on my precious carpet."

He did as told, now towering over her instead, nearer than he'd ever gotten to her, their faces so close she merely needed to raise herself on her toes to press her lips to his jaw. A thought that shook her awake quicker than a bucket of cold water and had her stumbling back for some space.

"There is a chair right here," he told her, bracing one hand on her chair and the other on her vanity table, trapping her between his arms.

She grabbed a hairbrush and pressed the other end to his chest, pushing him back with it. "Out, Gabriel."

He looked down between them as he walked backwards towards her door. "Resorting to weaponry. Very unfair of you, my pretty ruin."

Frustrated breaths entered Silene's lungs. "Don't call me that."

"As you wish, my beautiful damnation."

Heat climbed up her neck, and she put a hand over it, hoping he'd not taken notice of what he'd done to her. "Not that either."

He stopped right at her bedroom doorstep, stretching his arms up and bracing both his hands on the top of the doorframe, reminding Silene just how massive of a man he was. "Tell me you've missed me."

Her lips parted for a quick breath. "I haven't missed you."

"Tell me you were hoping I'd come to you."

"I have not," she might have lied.

"Tell me you don't hate me again."

Her limbs were growing so very soft under his burning perusal. "I think I'm starting to change my mind about that."

"Then tell me you do," he said, his eyes dropping to her mouth, the blue of his irises invaded entirely by his dark pupils until they remained a thin ring of sapphire. "I should probably tell you," he breathed, his chest rising and falling fast, "that I was hoping you'd call for me. I waited. I was going to wait, I swear it. But something told me you might never call for me. Be cruel to me all you want, I've given you that right. But what cruelly have those poor flowers committed to you to leave them to wither without a drop of water?"

She briefly pressed the back of her hand to her mouth to hide her smile. "They are watered only every two to three days. Even less here in Asphodel because we don't really have any sun."

His lips parted, and he slowly nodded. "I see. I might have killed your flowers."

"I know."

Gabriel looked a little stunned at her admission. "You should have stopped me."

"It was too funny."

"So, you were watching me."

Forcing her amusement away, she said, "Out, Gabriel."

His eyes gleamed as he backed away down her stairs, grinning and almost tripping because she was sure every ounce of his attention was on her. "You were watching me."

"You were in my garden. Intruding."

"And you were watching me."

She stared at the shop's display window, her mouth parted open with fascination, her eyes almost welling from excitement as she braced both hands on the glass barrier, trailing her fingers down the details on the white dresses on the mannequins.

Gabriel stepped beside her. She could feel his questioning gaze dripping down on her like warm wax as he silently watched her admire the wedding dresses. He'd obeyed her first demand that he was to take her to visit a bridal store—breaking her rule of never stepping on human spaces yet again.

To her luck, he had not asked for any explanation for her demands, only had followed after her like some pup on a leash.

The store was strangely empty as they got inside, and she turned to him. "There is no one here."

He sat by a large sofa probably meant for guests, his arms spread wide on the back rest. "Try some of them on."

She blinked, flustered. "I only wanted to see."

"The store is all ours for today. Try some and show me. I want to see."

Silene did not need to be told twice. She skimmed the long rows full of silk, lace, and all kinds of dresses hung along the walls, stopping only to pull a few out and hang them over her arm.

She'd never undressed faster, her clothes discarded all over the changing room as she quickly stepped into the first dress, cursing when she realised she needed to be zipped in.

Poking her head out of the changing room, she met his gaze and sighed. "I need help."

With a huge grin, he got up and stepped right behind her, gently pushing her hair to one side, careful not to touch her as he reached for the zipper and slowly pulled it up.

She couldn't look away from his reflection on the mirror before her when his eyes lifted to meet hers and then travelled down her body. She wanted to look away, to look at the dress that fit her as if it had been made for her. No matter how much she tried, she couldn't look away at all, too entranced by the way his blue irises turned molten at her sight.

"Why wedding dresses?" he asked, his fingers grazing the very ends of her long hair, curling around them, the sensation sending a shudder down her spine.

"I've always wanted to be a bride," she said, tracing the beads on her bodice. "When my father would drink too much, I would sneak and hide behind a grand oak by the temple in our village, watching brides walk down the long aisle to the sound of the chiming bells. I'd seen nothing more beautiful, it was entirely out of a dream. Like the fairies I'd read about when I was younger."

"Did you ever want to get married?" he asked.

Her bitter chuckle filled the empty hall, and she pressed a shaky hand to her mouth to muffle the sob that threatened to follow when memories of her old life returned. "Who would have wanted to marry me? My name was tainted with more than just poverty," she admitted. "People knew, you know. They all knew what was happening to me." They all knew what was being done to her. Some were their own wives, their own daughters and sons, their own parents. And instead of turning that scrutinising glare on their own kin, they had turned it on her. She'd been cast out, spit on, hit on, hated on, even denied any service by the villagers—if she'd been on fire, no one would have wasted a drop of water on her.

The tip of his finger traced the length of the silver zipper on her spine, and that was the closest he could get to touching her. "And they've all paid for it."

Silene almost didn't hear his words because of how low his voice had gotten. "What did you say?" she asked, looking up at him, noticing the tight features, the shadows, and the drowning eyes.

"Put your hair up."

She blinked fast. "Why?"

"Just do it."

Gabriel stood rooted there behind her as she did as he'd asked, pinning her long hair at the base of her neck, all too lost watching him watch her to realise that the scar on her neck was now all for him to see.

Only when his eyes in the reflection dropped down from hers did she realise.

A hand came to rest there under her neck, covering it. "Would you stop looking at me?"

"*Gods* and *Fates* have tried, and they both have failed to make me do so. But you can give it a try, too, my pretty desolation." He stepped even closer, his chest almost brushing her back but not quite so when he leaned into the naked crook of her neck and closed his eyes. "You smell like heaven."

Ignoring the chill that chased down her limbs, she said, "Didn't know the heavens had a smell."

"Mine does."

"Also didn't know you owned one. But then, you seem to own many things."

"I don't own her," he said, reaching for a veil and pinning it at the back of her head. "But she does own me."

"You're a pathetic God."

"You have no idea, Silene," he muttered, trailing the tips of his fingers down the long veil. "Are we keeping this one or will you try another one on for me?"

Her eyes went wide. "I can keep it?"

"Why not?"

She contemplated it for a moment, trying to bite her smile down as she studied herself in the mirror, the pretty high neckline decorated with pearls and sparkles and the long silky train that followed the curves of her body, floating and pooling down at her feet. She looked like one of the women from the human magazines. "Fine, thank you. Will you unzip me?"

"Keep it on."

A ridiculous laughter left her. "I'm not walking around in a wedding dress."

They stepped outside the shop and into the streets. Silene giggled at herself the whole time they walked, spinning in her dress and fluffing the veil around until a kid gasped and pointed straight at her. "Mommy! A princess!"

Ice cold water washed over her skin, her smile fading, and she almost hid behind Gabriel. "Why...why can he see me? He's not dead."

"Pretty things should be seen, Silene."

He'd made her visible. After five hundred years, humans could see her again. And that thought...did not scare her as much as she had thought it would. "I'm in a wedding dress. I look ridiculous."

"You look exquisite."

If her face had not gone red from embarrassment, it surely had done so from his frustrating words. "Gabriel."

"Yes, my Silene?" he asked, standing right in front of her and pulling the veil down her eyes. "There. Now no one can see you. You're invisible again. Now come."

How did he know how to soothe her so well? Even from before when he'd been just a flame in a candle. "The river is the other way around."

"We will make a stop somewhere else before."

"A stop? Where?"

A chapel stood before them after a few turns around the buildings and many pointed looks later. Small, hidden between two massive buildings like a tattered, forgotten book in a library shelf between brand new ones.

"Why did you bring me here?" she asked, studying the decor as he led her inside.

"You're in a wedding dress. It would be such a pity to waste this opportunity," he said, backing away towards the altar that was lined with seats, and standing right at the spot where the groom usually waited for the bride. "Walk to me, Silene," the odd God called for her.

Her heart had pooled down her stomach, pulsing so violently that she almost felt sick. "I can't...we can't."

"It's all pretend. It's all it can be anyway. Pretend. What's the worst that can happen?"

Silene could think of a thousand terrifying things that could happen if she did. Still, she took a step forward.

With a swift flick of his hand, the grand organ piano played the tune every human bride walked to in this realm. Another flick of his hand and white roses bloomed through the walls, over the benches, along the altar, hanging overhead into arches, their thorned vines twisting around anything and everything, turning the chapel into something of a sweet, perfumy dream. And as he raised his hand in her direction, beckoning her to him, a swift yet gentle wind swept across, snowflakes pouring out of the roof of the closed chapel, bright crystals gleaming as they fell on her dress, on the flowers, and the red carpet. She smiled when the cold flakes touched her lips, coated her lashes, and turned the tip of her nose a little red, her cheeks probably, too.

She fixed her veil as she closed the distance between them, a bouquet of white flowers appearing in her hand, withering almost immediately from her touch. Despite it, this was the most magnificent thing she'd ever been part of, and better than any daydream of hers.

He stood there, too, just like a dream, just in jeans and a black t-shirt instead of the ornate suit grooms usually wore. This time not faceless either.

"How did I do?" she asked, stepping in front of him.

He reached for her veil, lifting it over her head and looking at her somewhat stunned, his chest rising fast. His lips parted and then closed again a few times, and she waited for the words that didn't come for a long while.

She jokingly smacked him in the chest with her dried and dead bouquet, chuckling. "You aren't so dashing yourself, your great grandness."

He reached to pull a lifeless flower from her bouquet, the carnation coming to life immediately at his touch. Silene jumped a little when he tapped the tip of her nose with it. "Liar, liar.

Pretty liar," he cooed, giving her one of his most charming grins and guiding the carnation he held over her cheek and then down her jaw, making her shiver and gasp, a puff of mist escaping from between her parted lips that were being kissed by flakes of snow.

He brought the flower down her chin, using it to gently lift her face up to him. "How do the vows go, my ruin?"

Silene did not wish to blink. Too scared it might all be just a dream, merely a dream. "All of them are different in every realm."

"Tell me your favourite."

She took a moment even though she knew them by heart, contemplating if she wanted to tell him such a precious secret. "Have my heart. Wounded, sick, or scarred. In your hands not stolen or gifted but surrendered. Became a half when it met yours, so in the eyes of Gods let it become whole again," she said, dropping her gaze from his and blinking in at her surroundings. "I think that's how it goes."

The flower he held to her face brushed the skin down her neck, and down her chest that rose faster and faster each passing second. The petals pressed between her breasts, right where her heart was pulsing hard enough to make her feel faint. "No one," he said in an almost whisper, "no one deserves that heart. I forbid you to offer it to anyone."

She was sure each pulse jumped over the other, every beat erratic as she stared up at him. "No one would have it even if I gave it to them for free."

"Smart little creatures humans are. To know of their worth. But wretched, for what they don't deserve, they have sought to ruin."

With some convincing, he'd managed to bring her to sit at a cafe, her veil pulled back this time as she sat on the other side of the small table, standing stiffly and turning away flustered when people would send glances her way. With her hands folded on top of the table, she looked like a painting stolen from a gallery, one painted with such craft that there was no eye who could admire her properly.

A server lowered a teacup in front of her and then another before me. "Congratulations to the both of you!" the girl said.

Silene opened her mouth to speak but the server was gone.

"Drink your tea, Silene," he said, hiding his smile behind his teacup, trying not to gloat too much at the fact that whoever was looking at them thought of her as his—as his bride.

She grabbed a spoon, clutching it tightly in her hand and looking like she was contemplating throwing it at him.

He chuckled. "Put the spoon down, my ruin. You can do more damage without it, should you wish to. Your words can bruise me better."

A flush stained her cheeks and ears, and she lowered her head, her hand closing around the teacup as she smiled down at it. Silene's eyes roamed around the cafe when she brought the cup to her lips and blew on the steam before taking a sip. "Never understood why people sit around like this. I guess it is nice having your tea made for you." She blinked at him when a long string of silence followed. "You haven't said a single word. Why did you even bring me here?"

"To stare at you and show you off."

Her lips parted, and she made to speak several times. He wondered why she was always looking for words in his presence.

"You're so beautiful, Silene. I wanted someone to think you're mine. Anyone. Even if only briefly."

Her hands let go of the teacup, returning to her lap, almost surrendered.

The server stopped at their table, a camera in her hand. "Could I take a picture of you?" She pointed to the wall where about a thousand other pictures of people drinking tea and coffee were plastered against. "For our wall. We've never had a bride come here. Let alone one that looks like you." The girl made a sound of awe as she studied Silene. "We would love to have you on our wall."

Silene shot him a panicked look, and when he nodded just once to assure her that all would be fine, she turned to the server, a careful smile upon her lips as she quietly said, "Of course."

Silene straightened her shoulders when the server lifted the camera to her face. Just before the flash snapped, her hazel eyes turned to him, silver lining them.

If she had not stolen enough of his breaths today, Gabriel stood there robbed of his very last one.

"Thank you!" the server chirped, waving over her shoulder at them.

"I'd like to go back," she said, standing, not looking at him anymore, not sparing him even a glance as they made their way to the boat that took her away from him every time. She did not even leave a goodbye.

Sat at the edge of his bed, long past midnight, he stared at the new frame in his hand, running a finger down the picture he'd trapped in it, the most precious thing he now owned. The first thing he'd done after he'd dropped her back to Asphodel, was to return to the cafe and ask for the photo. He could not even make himself look away ever since it had been placed in his hands.

Sat there in her white dress, staring away from the camera, staring at him, the saddest yet happiest he'd ever seen her be.

"My taunting eidolon, my lovely apparition, my beautiful phantom," he murmured as a tear fell against the glass frame. "How many more nights must I mourn you?"

Seven o' Clock

AZRIEL STOOD ACROSS LETHE River, arms crossed over his chest and eyes narrowed on Gabriel who lifted a hand and waved his fingers at him, wearing the biggest grin he could muster. A grin he was finding hard to hide after his letter this morning.

Wear something pretty for me, he'd written to her.

Only if you wear something pretty for me, she'd said back.

When he spotted Silene sprinting down the hill in his direction, he even threw his brother a wink.

"You think you've won over *Fates* just because she now comes to you willingly?" Azriel asked him.

"The fuckers can go fuck themselves."

"Don't do that, brother. If not for the sake of you, for the sake of her."

"Not a hair on her pretty head will be touched in death or in any life, that I can promise you."

He shook his head. "How do you ever plan on making sure of that?"

"Threatening and begging. Loads of it."

"You think the *Fates* will listen?"

"Fuck them," he said, and then added, "I've got friends in high places, baby brother. Many of them. Why do you think I've made a bargain with each and every God in these past five hundred years? They all owe me. You owe me, too, remember? Once she leaves your kingdom, every single one of them will make sure she lives like a God amongst humans. And in death shall she come again, here too she will be a God. You will make sure of it." He tilted his head back, regarding his quiet brother. "Winter, wasn't that her name?"

Azriel stiffened, and the skies on his side of the river darkened at the mere mention of the human woman who his brother had left his heart with. "Don't."

"Worry not brother, I mean no harm to her. I went through enough shit to find someone who can even tolerate your prickly ass. And for that you owe me."

"You think she will still come to you when she finds out the truth?" his brother asked, and in turn, the skies over his own side darkened.

Silene stopped beside Azriel, forcing Gabriel to seal his mouth shut. She handed him her *timekeeper* and patted his shoulder. "Consider this a holiday notice."

Gabriel's grin faded into a sneer when his brother turned to him, smirking as he pushed his glasses back with a finger, gloating at the fact that she could touch him. "Call if you're sick of his unbearable arrogance, I will send someone for you."

Silene waved over her shoulder as she crossed the bridge between life and death, almost running into his arms if he'd not caught himself and taken a step back. "What did you pick out of the list today?" she asked, giving him a little uncomfortable smile as if to deter him from what had almost happened.

"A surprise," he said, bringing a rose from behind him and brushing the soft petals against her cheek and down her jaw before offering it to her to take.

"It will die," she said, hiding her hands behind her back.

"All things die, Silene. All living things wish they could die by gentle hands. This rose will have the gentlest, kindest death of all. A mercy to wither in your hold."

He saw her swallow, and the way she regarded him with such

desperate, woeful eyes as she reached for the flower, already knowing its fate, made his heart ache like never before.

The moment she held it, the stem began turning a pale shade of brown, drying out and dying, the petals turning stiff and a dark grey. She brought the rose to her nose, a feigned smile gracing her face. "At least it still smells good."

He brought a folded piece of ribbon from his pocket, unfolding the silky black material and holding one end of it while handing the other end to her. "There will be a crowd where I'm taking you, and I don't want to lose you in it."

Silene reached for the other end, wrapping her fingers around it, and this was the closest they could ever come to holding hands. She followed after him as he stepped across the veil between life and death, right into the middle of a bright, loud, and massive theme park—her second demand.

"Can they see me?" she asked, clinging close to him, as close as she could, and Gabriel contemplated lying to her.

"Only if you want them to."

"You will look insane talking to nothing."

"You're worried about me?"

"Never mind," she said, unravelling her hand from her ribbon and stepping back from him. "Make me invisible."

"As you wish, my ruin," he said, tugging on the ribbon they held onto and bringing her close to him again.

They stopped before a massive ferris wheel, waiting in line, and he could feel the dread dripping off her as she stiffly stood at his side, staring down at her boots. From the way her chest rose and fell, he could tell panic had gripped her.

"Silene," he called to her, and she turned to him. "They can't hurt you. They can't even see you."

Panicked tears clung to her lashes. "Why does it not feel like that?"

At the snap of his fingers, everyone disappeared, the rides grew quiet, the air settled, the laughter faded, as did the line before them. "Come," he said, tugging on the ribbon.

She still stared wide eyed at him as they sat beside one another in the small cabin.

At another snap of his fingers, the ferris wheel started moving again.

"Where did everyone go?" she asked, looking out of the window and searching the massive amusement park as they were being raised higher and higher off the ground.

"There was no one there to begin with. You keep asking where people are every time I take you somewhere, and I thought...you might think of this as excessive."

"It is a bit." She went quiet for a moment, and then lifted their hands still clutching the ribbon. "So, this wasn't even necessary at all?"

"It is."

Her brow arched. "Thought you didn't want to lose me in the crowd."

"There was a crowd."

Her eyes narrowed. "There isn't one now."

"You might fall."

She chuckled but did not let go of the ribbon. "Sure."

"Why did you want to come to a theme park?"

Silene leaned against the open ledge, looking over the park and the city lights on the horizon. "Saw it in those human magazines. It was in an article called '*Ten things to do before you die*'." She sighed. "I can see what they mean. It is beautiful up here."

"It really is," he said, looking at her.

Her gaze turned shy. "You're not even looking."

"I'll trust you on it."

She shifted in her seat, throwing him a couple careful glances. "I don't think I like heights all that much."

Gabriel reached inside his jacket pocket and brought out a small metal flask, handing it to her. "Any other realisation while we are at it?"

"Like what?" she asked, taking a small sip, and wincing at the taste.

"That you find me irresistibly handsome."

She huffed. "I find you irresistibly annoying."

"And handsome," he said, and Silene's attention dropped to the flask when he pressed his lips where hers had been just seconds ago. "You know I don't mind you looking at me, so no need to do it all so secretly."

Her eyes rolled. "Put me down."

"Always trying to run away from me, my ruin."

She scooted a bit further away from him. "I will jump, Gabriel."

"I wouldn't let you."

"You can't touch me."

"I will stop the very earth from spinning if I have to."

"You closed me up here on purpose," she said, her voice low like a bewitching spell to Gabriel's ears.

"So evil, aren't I?" he asked, bracing an elbow on the seat rest and leaning closer to her, just looking at her and marvelling at the colours her hazel eyes took from the setting sun behind them. "I'd do terrible, terrible things to have you this close all the time."

Those haunting eyes of hers paced between his, and her hands curled over the fabric of her skirt. "You selfish God," she whispered.

"My pretty Reaper," he hummed, bringing a finger just under her chin and watching her shiver when he ghosted it up and down her jaw.

Her soft voice was low, so low when she said, "Fool."

"I am. What else? Tell me what else?"

She swallowed, looking away and making his heart race with so much anguish. "I want to try the spinning thing. With the animals."

There were rides after rides after that. Most of which she hated beside the carousel and the ferris wheel.

"I'll take it back," she said, nibbling on some cotton candy and licking her fingers, a massive bear tucked under her arm. "I don't see why humans would want to do all this before they die."

He stole some of her cotton candy. "Not enjoying it?"

"It was a nauseating experience. I don't know why anyone would enjoy the need to feel sick and dizzy. The most thrilling part of it all was the contemplation of whether I was going to hurl at you or not after that last spin."

Gabriel chuckled. "How about I take you down to the sea?

He knew he'd said the right thing when her face lit up.

Sat at the edge of a cliff overlooking the ocean, he watched Silene in his leather jacket that had swallowed her limbs entirely, her eyes closed, and the smallest of smiles lingering on her face as she let the sea wind beat at her, carrying her long, silky hair in dark waves. "I love the wind," she said. "I think I do. I don't really remember even regarding it before."

Gabriel didn't speak. Not a single word. He didn't wish to ruin this memory of her, the first thing so close to what humans called a religious experience.

With a sigh, she laid on her side, resting her head on the bear toy he'd won for her. Facing him, she curled onto herself on the grey rock they'd perched on to witness the new turn of day. Her lashes fluttered slowly, almost lulled by sleep, but she seemed to refuse to give in.

No colour had ever mattered to Gabriel. Colours were just colours.

But her eyes. Oh, her eyes.

The moment he'd looked into them long ago, every existing thing had held a breath with him in acquiescence. He was sure nothing to ever graze any realm, space and nook in the vast universe could replicate that very same colour. He remembered the very first thoughts that had crossed his mind back then. That he wanted to bottle it, to make it an elixir for the unexplainable heartache it had given him.

She lifted a hand up, her shadow on the ground mimicking her as she made nonsensical shapes with her fingers that had her grinning from ear to ear and her eyes glowing with such fascination that Gabriel could not understand.

Her smile suddenly fell, and he turned to look at what had been at fault. Her shadow was touching his. The tip of her finger traced his silhouette on the stone. "You're the only thing that doesn't die by my touch," she said.

He lifted a hand, letting the cast of its shadow graze hers, the tips of their fingers meeting on the stone. "And you're the only thing that dies by mine."

Silene took one long breath and tucked her hands to her stomach. "Maybe you should take me back now."

"Maybe I should keep you for myself."

She looked up at him. "I'm not yours to keep."

"Who'd stop me?"

Gabriel knew he'd won whatever battle *Fates* had started years ago when she thought about it for a minute. "Azriel."

His smile was uncontainable. "Does that mean you're up for keeps if he didn't exist?"

"That sounded like a very vague threat to your brother."

"It was."

She slammed her boot on his, shaking her head. "You love him. I know you do."

"I do," he admitted, a little afraid that some vengeful deity or *Fate* might have heard him.

"You show it so little."

"I shouldn't be showing it at all considering how I was taught to regard him by our parents."

Silene frowned at him. "You're a powerful God, you should be able to love however you like."

"One would think so," he said, reaching to pull away the wind billowed hair from her eyes.

"Why does everyone hate you?"

"Impossible. This is news to me," he said, chuckling.

She reached for the edge of his t-shirt, playing with the material, and Gabriel's chest nearly burst. "You've made an enemy out of every God and Goddess."

His attention was on her fingers tracing the trim of his shirt. "Because every single one of them has wanted something from me and were upset they could not take it without exchanging it for something else."

"The bargains," she mused.

"The many, many bargains."

She winced. "You could just be nice and help them."

"I can't compensate fate with *nice*. To give, you have to take.

They all know that."

She pulled her hand back to her stomach. "So, you'd rather be hated?"

"Their regard does not matter to me, Silene."

"Nor your brother's?"

He shook his head. "Nor his. It doesn't matter. I will always love him no matter what. No matter his hate or the destiny we were born to follow."

"Sounds lonely."

"It is the life I was born to lead."

"You've never struck me as someone who accepts their fate."

He looked away into the ocean distance. "To keep those I love safe, I would have accepted a life in a secluded box floating in the universe aimlessly."

"Who else has seen your world? Visited your home for terrible tea, met Tommy, been taken out to theatres and cafes?"

"Only the one that mattered."

Silene rolled on her back and her eyes became a mirror for the cloudy skies above. "You should meet more people."

"Not interested in meeting any people."

"You should visit Az a little more frequently. You can stop by my home for tea."

"Is it an invite?"

"It's permission. I won't be here soon." Her chest rose fast, furiously, while his own collapsed entirely. "Tommy likes people. Let him meet more people."

"Silene—"

"I know you're eternal and have all the time in the world, but you should let people in. You have so much to give and no one to give it to. It isn't all so unpleasant being around you either."

"No?"

Her eyes drew shut, her voice drowned by sleep when she murmured, "Not at all actually."

Eight o' Clock

SILENE STILL WASN'T QUITE so used to seeing the God of Life
sitting at her kitchen table, trying the sweet goods she had baked
all night long because she couldn't sleep at all thinking about his
ridiculously handsome face, imagining running her fingers over
his mouth, down his nose, over his eyes, through his hair. Suddenly overpowered with a strange sensation that vaguely reminded her
of grief. She felt as if she was leaving someone else behind—one
she could not take with this time.

Cupcakes and cookies of all shapes lined the kitchen counter,
while the rest of the cakes were resting by the windowsills, cooling
for her to put frosting on.

From time to time, she raised her gaze from her buttercream,
looking at him. Only looking away because the urge to do as she'd
imagine all night long grew unbearable.

"You still haven't told me the occasion for all of this," he said,
licking some frosting from his finger and then running his tongue
over his lips as he leaned back on her kitchen chair, giving her his
full attention.

"No occasion."

His brows lifted up as he took in all the desserts crowding her kitchen. "Not opening a bakery? Catering a birthday? Feeding at least five impoverished nations?"

"I bake for fun."

"You don't look like you're having fun," he said, standing and bracing his hip on the counter right next to her. "You look distressed."

Clamping her lips shut, she turned to beat her buttercream until her arm almost fell off.

Something cool rested under her chin, and she jolted when she looked down at the tip of a butter knife against her skin. Gabriel used it to gently turn her head in his direction. "I'm not beyond slaying any demon, human or not, if you ask me to, my ruin. Just ask me. Tell me what is hurting you and I will hurt them back two-fold."

Silene was so confused. So very confused. Terribly confused. Why her? Why? What in the cruel, cruel name of *Fates* was happening? What did this mean?

Swallowing, she said, "You can't slay time."

A devilish smirk rose on his lips. "I wouldn't be quite so sure."

Her eyes roamed all over his face, and she realised why she found so much comfort in his eyes. Skies, seas, lakes, and rivers, that's what they reminded her of. "Shouldn't you be the pacifist of all Gods? The most docile of them all?"

"What about me is docile? My power is violent, perhaps the most violent of all. Uncontrollable. It can grow a flower as it can grow a tumour. It can bring hope as much as it can bring ruin. Once life takes root, I no longer possess any control over it, it can either bloom or rot. The purpose of my existence was to give life, not to control it." He dipped his finger on her buttercream and brought it to his lips, licking it off. "Weren't you the one to tell me that I've never been the good guy? I'd rather you don't grow fond of me, my desolation."

"Fond is not the word I'd use." She had not lied. It was something akin to fascination, perhaps addiction, too. There was something eminently...moreish about him. His presence was all too light, like moonlight. Gentle, not blazing or burning like sunlight, but featherlight and effulgent. Longing would strike upon you when you least expected it. Like rain on long and hot summer days. You would not realise how much you missed it until the dried earth mourned for a drop.

"What word would you use then?" he asked, using the butterknife again to turn her attention back to him.

She'd never wished more that it was his fingers resting on her chin instead. Silene had never known how it felt for someone to crave her attention—and she was not entirely sure she hated it. "How am I your ruin?"

The question seemed so simple. Yet he took a while to answer her. Only for it to be no answer at all.

"What am I to do, Silene?" he asked, his eyes eating her whole. "This buttercream is fucking heaven. Your buttercream has ruined all buttercreams for me. I might hollow out and vanish if I don't have this buttercream every single day. I will dream about this buttercream. And every time I go past pastry shops, I will long to see this buttercream on all the cakes."

She grabbed a mitten and threw it at his face. And a tea towel. And then a ladle. And a few more other stuff as she chased him out of her kitchen. By the time she had him out of her door, he was keeling over from laughter, holding a few of her cupcakes that he'd collected on his way out.

"Leave before Azriel comes and kicks your ass out."

He threw her a wink. "See me later. Preferably not only in my dreams."

She gagged. "Ugh."

"Not the sound I'd love for you to make, but I'll take it."

She raised a middle finger, and he puckered his lips, blowing her a kiss, sealing their battle zero to one in his favour.

Two deaths had been left for her to collect after the one she'd just sent off to Asphodel.

She'd done it with such mellow steps, almost tempting *time*, almost provoking the unforgiving Goddess. From time to time, she'd glanced over her shoulder, hoping Gabriel would interfere. That kind of hope had left her with the bitterest taste in her tongue, and she'd quickly sent the soul back to Asphodel, not even waiting for a second boat, afraid he'd find her if she stood too long in one stop. So, she'd circled the small city of Asador round and round until she was sure she'd confused *Fates* themselves to the point she'd rewritten destiny.

Just as she was about to cross the street towards the invisible bay where a boat was now finally waiting for her, a silver car stopped right at her feet for some reason, the windows rolling down the passenger side. "Why are you hiding from me, Silene?" Gabriel asked, leaning in the passenger seat to look up at her.

"I'm not hiding."

"If I can't find you, it means you are hiding," he threw her own words back at her.

"I need some space."

His brows pinched with confusion. "Fine, pick a few stars or whatever else, and I will get them for you, what is the big fuss?"

She rolled her eyes. "As in distance." Pointing between them, she added, "Between us."

That look of confusion deepened in his face. "There's always space between us, so get in the car."

"No."

"Get in the car, Silene."

She got in the car, making sure to stomp and slam her way in, refusing to let down her feigned wall of indignation that was now paper thin and no longer keeping him away. "Where are you taking me?"

He lifted her folded paper between his two fingers. "Three more demands to go."

"What's the rush?" she asked, biting the inside of her cheek raw, only stopping when she felt the taste of blood on her tongue. A thousand thoughts crossed her as she held her breath, wondering if it had happened because she was so close to paying her debt to Azriel or because she'd gotten so close to Gabriel and therefore closer to getting a taste of her old humanity back.

Like the devil he was, he flashed her another of his sinful smirks. "I can take it slow, Silene. As slow as you want, my ruin. Come here," he beckoned her, and for whatever reason that would not come to her at that moment, she leaned in. Her lashes fluttered fast when he leaned in, too, his lips so close to her neck. So very close she shivered as if he'd pressed them against her skin.

And when he breathed her in and exhaled, a tendril of tender, warm fire licked a path down her chest, teasing every curve and dip on the way until it pooled into a burning hearth between her legs. It was such a strange sensation to Silene. So new. So forbidding.

"So sweet, my ruin, you smell so sweet." He lifted a hand to her face, the tips of his fingers just ghosting down her jaw. "I've been trying all day to recall your perfume. I was growing afraid I'd gotten it wrong. I don't want to forget it."

No one—nothing at all had ever made Silene feel as she did by mere words alone, by their mere breath on her skin, by their mere presence so near her.

Silene had never...never wanted to be touched as much as she had wanted that very moment. And as she stood there with that realisation, another settled in. Nothing had ever wanted her back.

When he lifted his head just a little to look at her, their lips gently brushed the other's. It was a touch as brief and gentle as the breeze, but Silene slammed her eyes shut, pulse beating hard against her neck, her temples, her chest. Her heart had never pulsed so furiously even when she'd been alive.

"Forgive me," he whispered, full of defeat, bracing his brow on her seat's shoulder.

Her fingers ghosted her bottom lip, wincing when they brushed against the new bruise there. "It's alright."

"It is not. It is not alright at all."

He only raised his head when she carefully and very gently brushed her fingers against his hair. It was a brief, tentative touch, but he looked at her as if he'd found salvation.

"I've always wanted to do that," she admitted. "It feels just like I imagined."

"What else have you imagined, Silene?" he asked, his voice almost drunken.

"Can't really say," she vaguely said to him, turning her body towards the window and chewing on her thumb as she stared at his reflection on the glass.

"You will tell me eventually," he confidently said, starting the car.

Her face was plastered against the window as they drove through the city, over a tall bridge and into the other side of the city where the buildings grew sparser, less tall, somewhat more colourful. The further in they went, the more greenery she could see. First it was just a couple trees, then whole gardens and flower filled pots scattered all over the front of the houses. Children loitered the streets, some on their bikes, others jumping on one foot on squares they'd drawn on the ground. The elderly had joined the young, too, some sat on their porches just watching life pass by, while others sat around a game board.

She turned to him. "You've never told me why you stay in this realm."

"It's only been a few years. I move from place to place."

"Why not settle like your brother?"

"I try to go where I'm most needed," he told her. "Where life of any kind grows sparser. It helps it grow back."

"Is that how you found me? Were you staying in my realm?"

There was a brief pause before he said, "No."

"How did you find me?"

"I stole a wish from a star."

She sneered at him. "If you don't want to answer me, just say so, you don't have to be a prick about it."

He dropped his head back on the head rest, grinning ahead as he drove them towards what looked like a hill, one entirely dressed in green.

Carefully, she threw some more glances at him. "You could have just snapped your fingers and taken us there."

"I thought you wanted to go slow?" he asked, slightly angling his head in her direction. "Besides, when you're in a rush, you tend to miss the beauty around you. Thought you might enjoy seeing the sides to humanity."

She took in a deep breath and exhaled a slow sigh as she watched the world go by. "Could never understand why anyone would choose to live out there when they could live here."

"Some live fast, Silene. Some live slow. Some live loudly, and some live quietly. Some have the choice, and some don't. Some like the company of others, some don't."

"It is pretty," she said, suddenly imagining herself living out there.

"As are you. Your new tablecloth suits you."

"Shut up," she muttered, dusting her long, brown skirt that she'd spent at least a couple months making.

He chuckled. "No one could ever pull it off like you do, my ruin. Not even a table."

Not wanting to give him the satisfaction, she shifted entirely on her side, hiding her smile.

The car stopped right at the foot of the hill, and Gabriel came to open her door, waiting until she was out before he grabbed a basket from the back seat.

"What's that?" she asked, squinting at him and putting a hand on her brow to shield her eyes from the harsh sun.

"A picnic basket."

She blinked once. "What's in it?"

"Food."

"What food?"

"Food I made," he told her like it was utterly normal.

Silene tried really hard to hold it in, but she could not resist the urge to laugh at the image before her. "All you're missing is a chequered apron, some red lipstick, and a perm, and you'd be the shining resemblance of those housewives from old human magazines."

His frown was low. "You need to stop reading that shit."

"They're entertaining." She rolled her shoulders back, wearing an expression of utter seriousness. "What have you prepared for us, dear wife?"

He shot her a look, one half amused and half a warning. "Done?"

"I'd smack you on the butt and tell you what a good little wife you are, but I don't want my hand to fall off," she giggled, following after him towards the green fields where many people had set camp to picnic. "You should have brought Tommy."

She watched as his expression fell just slightly. "He isn't entirely himself lately. I didn't want to tire him."

A sense of gloom settled in her stomach. "Oh. He'll be okay," she offered, joining his side.

"Yeah," he replied, voice weak. "Yeah, he will. Both of you can't leave me at once." His smile trembled. "What a cruel joke it would be."

She'd laughed to her heart's desire when he'd started laying a blanket down under the shade of a grand willow tree and neatly placed food out on a tray. Her imagination was not rich enough to have ever conjured a more outlandish scenario than the one before her. "You should have tried a wedding dress the other day. Would have been such a lovely bride."

"Glad I can make you laugh, my ruin," he said, making her smile turn shy all of the sudden.

She cleared her throat and sighed, observing the world around her move and bolster alive with such a violence that she had never witnessed, such vibrance she did not know it existed. Children were screaming, running, playing, and laughing. Adults were chatting and shouting to their kids to be careful. Birds and crickets were composing their own melodies, somewhat matching each other's tunes. The willow branches hissed and floated in tender waves as the gentle wind picked them up, letting the sun sieve through them. Silene found a fervent urge to hum along that sound and reach a hand out to play with the strands of sunlight peeking through between the branches.

Resting her chin on her knees, she smiled, drunken from the spring air that was filling her lungs with more than just oxygen, with something else, with something equally peaceful as it was violent, something akin to...hope. With hope that it would be better. That everything would be alright. That she should not fear. It terrified her just as much as it pacified her.

"Why did you stop?" Gabriel asked.

"Something was missing. A sound was missing."

"What sound?"

His voice.

Turning, she rested her cheek on her knee and looked up at him. "I love the sun. And the moon. I love yellow. And lilies. The wind and the sea, oh I love the sea. Cold wind, too. I love winter, but only when it is not raining. Spring is my favourite. I love spring. But mostly I just love the sun," she confessed. "Azriel once told me to make a list of what I missed from back when I was alive. Besides my brother, I could not recall anything else. Now I can give him a list." She waited a moment. "The lilies. It was you, wasn't it?"

For a few seconds, he just looked back at her, his eyes pacing between hers. "Would you hate them if I said yes?"

She'd doubted. She'd doubted for so long it had been because of him. "Why?"

"I didn't know how to bring you out of your house. You'd never leave it. Only would sit on a window and watch outside of it."

"How did you do it? Something like me isn't able to touch without killing."

"I bargained."

An anxious flutter settled in her chest. "And my dreams? You got my nightmares to stop a couple weeks ago."

His mouth twitched. "You knew it was me?"

"You told me to have sweet dreams. And I did. What did you bargain for them?"

"Nothing of importance," he lied to her, and lifted a plate full of some sweet treats to her. "Have one."

"I don't have to eat," she said, watching the strawberries dipped in chocolate laid out with a pang of disappointment.

"Doesn't mean that you can't."

"They will surely taste like nothing."

Grabbing a strawberry, he held it up to her mouth. "You will never know unless you try."

Reluctantly and very slowly, she leaned forwards, her teeth digging on the fleshy fruit, and she paused, rolling her eyes up at his that were watching her with such smouldering attention.

It was sweet. It was the sweetest thing she might have ever tried.

He then lifted a spoonful of sweet, flavoured yoghurt to her, and she opened her mouth again, letting him feed her, and watching as he brought the same spoon back to his mouth and licked the rest of it clean. "So?"

"Sweet," was all she could say.

Satisfied, he grinned at her and laid down, stretching on the blanket.

Silene glanced at the people a small distance away from them running around with strings tied to kites carried by wind so high they were about to disappear between clouds. It wasn't the only thing she noticed though. So many eyes were in their direction, but they were not on her. Everyone was looking at the *God* laying down beside her with his hands under his head and his eyes closed, his black shirt pulled up to reveal a sliver of skin on his stomach that was covered in tattoos like the rest of his limbs were. "Finally see something you like?" he asked, smirking.

"Women and men look at you like they want to have you."

He flashed her a wolfish grin. "Who would not?"

She huffed. "I've watched humans complain enough to know that arrogant men are always lousy lovers."

"Perhaps."

She was stunned at his admission. "Perhaps?"

"It has been so long."

"Since what?" she asked, grabbing another strawberry.

"Since I've been anyone's lover. Five hundred and something years to be exact."

Silene stopped chewing her strawberry, the sweet fruit suddenly tasting sour against her tongue.

Taking advantage of her distraction, he sat up and leaned in to bite the rest of the strawberry she was holding between her fingers, his lips almost grazing her skin. "Celibacy has not been half as bad," he said, licking his lip and standing there, his face merely inches away from her. "First, the object of my desires tends to hide from me. And I can say it with full confidence that it hasn't been much of a struggle. Especially when I spent half of that time imagining her to be in love with my brother and the other half of it contemplating what I could give to be able to just touch her."

Silene swallowed, the world around her suddenly starting to

spin too fast, so fast that she grew dizzy. "Don't speak," she breathed, her words burning.

"Forbid me."

"Gabriel—"

"Have I told you," he said, moving her billowing hair out of her face with the gentility of the wind. "How much I love how you say my name? Like you wish to gut me and eat me alive. I'd let you feast on every single bone. I'd let you pull me apart however you'd like."

She shook her head, her breaths stuttering and choking. "Why? You never tell me why? Why won't you tell me anything at all?"

"You would not understand. You would never understand if I told you how my soul has been forever tied to yours in ways no soul should ever be tied to another's," he said, his eyes dropping to her mouth. "For a while, I could not even understand myself. I couldn't understand anything at all. I had to make peace with the fact that I'd be longing for you forever before I even knew why."

She whispered, "That does not sound nice at all."

"If I could steal anything—anything at all," he breathed, "I'd steal just a kiss from your lips."

Harsh wind swept across the hill as she sucked in a breath before saying, "I would have given it to you."

Slowly, his head lowered and his eyes drew shut, as did hers, for there was finality in their fates—a finality she still did not entirely understand.

Why would they both be sentenced to such a fate? What had they ever done to deserve it?

He walked beside her as they retreated back to his car close to the day's near end, the doomed two feet space between them somehow growing vast, deeper than any canyon or river or sea. The longer she remained there, just two feet from him, the further she felt from him.

So Silene inched closer and closer with each step they took, and unlike the many other times when that space between them had been breached, she didn't feel weak at all. If anything, Silene felt unbeatable. Perhaps it is why she did what she did next.

Her pinkie brushed his, and she heard him suck a sharp breath. "Silene—"

Before he could even finish saying her name, she slid her hand against his, linking their fingers together. She only felt him for a fraction of a second before her entire body was possessed by pain. Tears clung to her eyelids as it raked through each muscle, bone, and sinew, carving its path deep inside the very core of her soul.

She still wouldn't have let go of him if he had not let go of her, backing away again to restore that wretched invisible isthmus between them.

He stared at her hand that had turned a rotten shade and almost gnawed to the bone. Terror changed the very blue of his eyes into an almost deep, dark sapphire. "Silene," he breathed, stricken with panic.

"It will go back to being fine when I return to Asphodel," she reassured him, pulling her lace scarf off and wrapping it around her unfeeling limb. "What would a ghost like me even need a hand for anyway?" She looked up at him just as a tear made its way down her cheek. "What's the point of even having one if I can't hold what I want to hold?"

Wind picked up, carrying his hair away from his brow and removing shade from the blue irises that had turned turbulent.

She reached a hand to her throat when those eyes dropped on the scar there, the scar she always hid.

"I should have obeyed the fates, I should have stayed away," he said, pressing a hand to his head and grasping at his hair. "At least I couldn't hurt you then."

A stab pierced her insides at his words. She wanted to tell him that she didn't mind. That her body could do nothing besides bruise and bleed. In fact, her body did it best. She bruised and bled like no other. So much so that her father had turned her into a spectacle for it. But why was he not laughing like her father and the monsters made of men had? Why was he staring at her as he was? Why had he never laughed?

"How am I even losing you?" he said, his mouth stretching into a trembling smile despite the tears in his eyes—tears that softened the very ground she stood on. Silene's world had never been shaken the way it did just then. "You were never even mine."

His.

Silene had never thought...she'd never thought she'd wanted to belong to someone. Someone who made her feel so light, so warm, who made her smile, who'd comforted her, who circled around her like the sun itself. Someone who had given sense to wind and rain, to rocks and clouds. Someone who'd made the entire world disappear for her.

One moment she was there, where she had always been, two feet apart from him. And the next, her arms were reaching over his shoulders, closing around his neck as she got on her toes and pressed her mouth to his.

Pain struck her across her chest first, grasping her heart in a firm, tight grip until she could barely breathe. But she'd been barely breathing for hundreds of years now so she paid no mind to it. How could she when his hands cupped her face and pulled her limp, pain ridden body to his firm one.

But her embrace was the place hopes went to die.

And he was wrenched away from her too suddenly. So suddenly that she swayed on her feet and almost took a tumble. Gabriel stood where he'd always stood, two feet away from her. But this time, he was watching her with a pair of wide and terrified blue eyes, breathing hard and fast.

Silene looked down at her hands, her arms, her chest, at the skin around them that had turned almost entirely grey, violet veins spreading all under her skin with blood that stung like poison. Everything came crashing in all at once. Realisation and pain alike. And she fell to the ground, her limbs struggling to hold her up. She didn't resist the call of weakness that lured her body to lay down on the cold, wet earth fresh from evening's dew.

And as her sight blurred, giving into the darkness, she saw him again, leaning over her, holding a shaky hand over her face. Silene had never witnessed such a storm, such angry skies and seas as the one in his eyes as he looked at her and shouted, screamed things she could not hear while her consciousness slowly dipped into darkness.

The next time she opened her eyes they were looking up at the wrong brother who was carrying her in his arms. "Where is he?" she asked, her own voice like blades against her throat.

Death did not look at her as he continued on his path to Asphodel, as he climbed the hill towards her home. "Gabriel will not come near you again."

"But I want him to. I was the one who got close."

He stopped, still not looking down at her though she was sure the scowl he directed at nowhere was meant for her instead. When he finally looked at her, there was nothing but pity in his gaze. And she'd never seen Death pity anything. "Do you know what that would mean, Silene?"

"I find very little meaning in things these days," she said, pushing at his chest and testing her feet. "I want to see him."

"I will not allow that," he said with a finality she'd not heard from him before.

"Az," she started, prepared to beg him, too.

"It is final," he said, vanishing.

Nine o' Clock

UNLIKE THE MANY PAST nights of light and steady rest, something had overtaken Silene's body, placing her into another world and letting her mind wander there. She'd been thrust back in her dark world of nightmares all of the sudden after she'd taste peace.

When she woke, the darkness had wrapped around her like a capsule, and the candlelight she always kept on had died. She patted the bed next to her, whimpering and crying as she hoped and prayed to everything and everyone that it had been just a dream, and that she was not back in her old body, laying beside someone who'd slowly been driving her to choose death.

As she frantically searched into the darkness of the room for monsters that would jump her without warning like they always did, pinning her down and violently taking what she did not give permission to be taken, her lips quietly shaped into the letters of his name. And they changed it like an incantation.

Gabriel. Gabriel. Gabriel. Gabriel. Gabriel. Gabriel.

"Please," she finally whispered at the end of her silent spell.

And the darkness answered. It answered for the first time ever.

"I'm here"

Silene sucked in a sharp breath, staring right ahead at the direction of that familiar voice despite not being able to see a thing. But she knew he could see her.

"What was it, my beautiful demise?" he asked.

Her voice was too small, too wounded by memories as she muttered, "Just a bad dream."

"What dares to worry you at night?"

Hugging her knees to her chest, she whispered, "Memories."

"Shall I take them? Shall I wrench them away and gut them apart one by one?"

"I don't know what I am without them," she admitted. "I don't know what I am without the violence."

"You're Silene. My beautiful Silene with the gentlest, kindest hands. It wasn't the violence that made you gentle, my ruin, it wasn't the violence that softened you. You were kind and soft and gentle despite it. You won over all. In spite of all, you won. They could not change you, nor your heart—your kind, gentle heart. And what they could not change they hurt. So let me take it away. Let me rip apart those memories for you."

Silene held onto that offer and his words like the most precious thing she'd owned. "Maybe...maybe I will let you take them away."

"You called for me," he said.

Her trembling lips parted as she confessed, "I did. But you were already here, weren't you?" She could smell the air scented with lavender, it had been what had dragged her out of nightmares.

"I was."

"For how long?" she asked.

"Since you fell asleep."

She bit into her smile. "That is disturbing."

A faint chuckle seeped into the darkness.

She sat up a little more, pulling the sheet to her chest when an unusual breeze swept from her open window, causing her to shiver and finally notice how very little she wore. "What were you doing in my room?"

"I had a question for you."

"Couldn't it wait?"

"The question could, but I couldn't," he said, dropping something on the table from the sound of it. "I had to see you."

"I can take a picture, so you don't have to come all the way here next time."

Though the room was in absolute darkness and Silene couldn't even see down her nose, she was entirely too sure he was grinning at her. "Of what kind?" he asked.

Her hand moved on its own volition as she grabbed the nearest pillow and threw it in his direction. Another faint chuckle following. "You can't stay here for this long," she regretfully said.

"What's the worst that can happen?"

"The universe could crumble. You're the greatest paradox in this land."

"Death sleeps. Fates sleep. Every existence there is sleeps. Only you and I are awake tonight." Silene jerked back when Gabriel's voice spoke directly in her ear instead of where he was supposed to be across the room. She had not imagined it. Because the moment she drew a deep breath, her lungs filled with his warm scent of lavender. "Do you know what I've done tonight, my ruin, to have just one moment with you? The waters I've poisoned, the air I've stolen, the stars I've bewitched, the Gods I've lied?"

"Gabriel—"

His name stuck to her lips when he pressed his own over them in a harsh kiss.

She was sure the whole universe had frozen. That time had vanished entirely. Maybe she was still in a cruel, cruel dream.

Especially when nothing happened. There was no pain. Not at all.

There was no pain when she kissed him back, or when her hands grasped his shirt to pull him to her, or when one of his hands cupped the back of her neck and the other banded around her waist to plaster her against him entirely. Seconds passed. Minutes passed. Maybe none at all. Their limbs had tangled with one another's, her fingers grasping his hair, and his fingers grasping hers as they kissed like two stars merging. She could not touch him enough and nor could he.

Gabriel pulled away only to ask, "Why did you kiss me?"

"Why did you?"

"Because," he murmured, nipping at her lips and slowly drawing another breath consuming kiss out of her. "I finally get to know how it feels to be alive."

Silene's chin quivered, her hands reaching to cup his face, and she relished how he felt in her hands, just as soft and strong and warm as she'd always imagined. "How?"

"If I tell you, I might scare you," he whispered back, pushing her hair behind her ear and pressing kisses all down her jaw before taking her lips again. "I don't want to scare you."

"I might scare you, too."

"There is nothing more I want," he said, lifting her onto his lap and letting her straddle his hips. "Make me afraid. Terrify me. I still have not made my peace with this fate. I don't think I ever will. So make me fear. Help me fear it for I know the pain will forever haunt me if I don't make peace with it. Tell me why did you kiss me."

Silene's heart had never broken as such before. Shattered to pieces. "I'm not scared of disappearing," she confessed, taking his hand and bringing it to her lips, kissing each knuckle and then his palm. "I couldn't think of a better way to vanish and leave nothing behind. Just like this. In your arms. Being held by you. It would be a dream. The dreams of dreams. I keep wondering how it would feel, this kind death I desire."

His sea-blue eyes turned silver with the shine of tears. "Nothing at all? No one at all?"

"Yes," she admitted, "nothing and no one."

"You heartless little thing."

She raised a hand to his face, feeling his skin under hers. "It would be better. Better than this." A cry slipped out of her. "The longing…it might kill me again."

"This is all my fault." His hand came to her face, his thumb moving over her cheek. "I did this."

"It couldn't be helped."

His eyes drew shut, and a pained look grasped his features that were drawn in shadows by the moonlight.

"You should go," she said with a heart so heavy it was weighing down to her stomach. "There is no point—no point at all to this."

"Please," he begged, but she didn't know what he was begging, or who. "Please."

Light suddenly filtered her room, and she could see the desperation in his eyes now, too.

"Take your hands off her and get out of here," a dark voice called from her doorway. Death stared at his brother and then at her, shaking his head at them both. "You cannot come and wreak havoc in my world, brother. You cannot come and confuse my people, weaken the land, weaken your own kin, your own brother!"

"She did it first," Gabriel said, burying his face on her neck, and making Silene turn red from the tip of her hair and down to her toes.

Azriel's nostrils flared, and he glanced around the room, his dark gaze fixing on a liquor bottle that did not belong to her. "You're drunk?"

Gabriel murmured something intelligible over her skin and then held her tighter, sighing and pressing his mouth all over her shoulder, her neck, her jaw.

"I will take him back," Silene said, trying not to shrink back under Death's harsh gaze or under the pain she was starting to feel now at Gabriel's touch that had weakened in his brother's presence.

"You cannot touch him outside of my world. You know I can't keep you safe out there."

"I can touch him for just a few minutes," she helplessly said.

"Silene," Azriel warned.

"I know." She gave him a quivering smile, tears filling her eyes. "I know." And she wasn't scared.

She was sure his already dark eyes went a shade even darker. "No, you don't. You cannot even begin to fathom the depths of chaos you would plunge into if he were to hurt you, the trial your souls could be put through if you cross the bounds of death. There are worse things than me in this universe, Silene. I suggest you do not tempt them." Death cocked his head back, his dark gaze shifting to his brother still holding onto her tighter than anyone had ever held her. "I will take him," he said with finality, stepping inside her room and attempting to peel his brother off her and failing. "Gabe!"

Her hand went to his hair, brushing the strands back and forth despite the painful rot starting to set in at the tips of her fingers,

"You have to go now," she murmured. "I will come and see you tomorrow."

"You will?" he asked, and she felt his tears roll down her shoulder.

"You have my word."

Then he was wrenched out of her arms like a band aid stuck to her fresh wounds, left there half bleeding, half torn, with no hope.

He'd been lied to.

Maybe not.

Maybe something had happened to her because of his reckless behaviour.

He could not even find out because his brother had done what he'd never done.

He'd closed the gate between life and death entirely, leaving him there desperate on the other side of the river while his ruin was right across, refusing to show herself.

Gabriel tried to not worry, reasoning that she was not an idiot like him. That when she worried she stayed home, busied herself and took care of anything that needed taking care of, and made pretty things out of the most unusual objects, she did not tempt the wrath of every God and Goddess, moon, star and sun there ever was, destiny and fate.

He almost jumped right up when her front door slowly drew open and she came out, wearing something strange—a yellow dress that fell just to the middle of her thighs that were bare except the tall black boots cutting at her knees. There was no scarf. Her hair was up in a long tail except the two white pieces dangling at the front.

Gabriel had been wrong. Silene was tempting—she was tempting him to commit things that would endanger every living thing there had ever existed.

"He's not letting me in," he said.

She came to a stop right at the very edge of the river. "Can you blame him?"

"Can't you take my side just this time?"

When she smiled, he realised she'd been on his side all along. "What did you do last night exactly?"

"Besides almost mauling you?"

She pressed her lips tightly together to hold in a smile that Gabriel almost begged to see, and then she nodded.

"Things I shouldn't have done," he confessed. "Things I didn't regret doing. Things I'm regretting doing now that I can't have you close." He waited for a few heartbeats, watching her head to toe, inspecting every visible inch of skin on her body. "Did I hurt you last night?"

Her teeth dug on the corner of her lip before she shook her head.

"Liar," he breathed.

She finally smiled at him. "It was nothing."

He started backing away, but she stepped on the bridge and crossed it before he could back away too far. Throwing a ribbon around his neck, she pulled on both ends to lower him to her before she said, "You're an absolute idiot."

He blinked. "Do you like idiots?"

"I don't mind them."

Gabriel smiled. "Good enough."

Pulling the ribbon off his neck, she wrapped one end on her hand and offered him the other. "You're still to take me to a zoo."

"You're always all business with me."

She glanced at him. "Are we taking it slow today?"

"As slow as you want to, my little bee. Are we stopping at your hive beforehand or straight to the zoo? Or is your hive there?"

She sneered at him. "I thought you liked yellow."

"I like *you*. Whether you make honey or not."

She'd fallen asleep in his car, still wearing the ridiculous hat and shirt they'd bought from the zoo's store, his jacket thrown over her lap. She lay on the passenger seat like a splatter of colour, a sight he thought he'd never see. A sight that made him so acutely happy it terrified him.

She stirred, peeling her sleepy hazel eyes to stare up at him. "Should you not take me back?"

"A few more moments. Time will not mind."

"Because you've made a bargain?"

"I'm a good businessman, what can I say?"

Silene reached for the monkey toy he'd bought her and squeezed its middle, making it release a few high-pitched sounds at his face. "I have the bear. You take the monkey. To remember me by."

He rubbed a shaky hand over his face that twisted with a cry before taking the stupid monkey. "You think I will ever forget you?"

"I hope you will," she said. "Eventually."

Ten o' Clock

Azriel remained quiet for a long while after her request.

A request she had never thought she'd ever make.

"Krune is no more, Silene," her oldest friend said.

She did not know what struck her first at the news of her old town's fate. Relief or sorrow. "How can a town be no more?"

"It might not be for me to say."

Dread pooled in her stomach. "I should have asked sooner. About my brother, too. About why I didn't see him when I arrived." She hugged her arms around her middle. "I was just hopeful it was a good sign that he wasn't. That he'd gone somewhere nicer, maybe been reincarnated already."

The quiet that fell between them had Silene's ears roar with noise of terror. "He did not die that day with you, Silene. He died a day later. Along with all of Krune. Then the entirety of your old realm followed."

Her feet swayed, and she braced her hand on the dark wall of his gloom filled home before she'd collapse. "What?"

"The poison you gave him did not take," he revealed.

No, Silene had made sure. Silene had made so sure he'd go

with her, she'd even used half her potion on him, too, so he'd go painlessly and faster than her even. "Then...then h-how did he die?"

Silene's spine steeled straight when he lowered his head and went quiet, her hand flying to her mouth to muffle her cries. What had she done? Had she left him in her father's hands?

The man who'd sold her the poison had promised it would be quick and that it would not hurt. Even though her brother had hurt all his life, hurt was all he had known, she had not wanted him to hurt in his last moments. She'd put more on his plate, so he'd leave without pain. She'd put her own half in his food, too, when she had fed him that one last meal that evening—a meal they had never had before, one she'd given too much in exchange of the little coin she'd gotten only to make sure her brother at least had one good meal before his death. "How did he die, Azriel!"

"It took the strength of many. Luke died a God." His dark eyes met hers. "He'd found out about everything that morning when he woke and you didn't. When he'd gone to bury you and been told the truth by a passerby. He died avenging you. I found him amidst many deaths, hundreds and thousands. But the blood spilled was owed to him for what those people had done to you, for what they had witnessed being done to you and remained quiet, so I left his soul behind, and someone else found him."

"W-Who?" she asked, a prayer more than anything—a prayer than nothing worse had found him.

"My brother," Azriel said, and Silene swayed on her feet. "Luke had prayed for him. To bring you back in exchange for the price of his own soul. A request my brother did not have the power to grant because—"

"Because what?" she asked. "Because what, Azriel!"

"Because I took you away from his reach forever."

Her hand went to her throat, to the scar that had once been a wound—her last wound. A wound she'd had to inflict upon herself after she'd woken at dawn sick to her stomach and realising her portion of the poison had not been enough to kill her. A wound she'd opened with the very same knife she'd cooked her brother his last meal. "Is it because I...because I—"

"No, Silene. It was because of him. He made a bargain with

me."

"A bargain? Gabriel made a bargain with you?"

Azriel nodded. "He did. And now he forever pays for it."

A bargain, Azriel's words whispered in her ear long after she'd left his home and travelled to a world she'd sworn to never step in, one she would not haunt. A world where Azriel had promised that her brother was happy. That was all Az had told her. She was to find out the rest—to piece the puzzle on her own.

Her feet remained rooted on the spot behind a tree trunk as she watched from afar a small wooden cottage surrounded by towering conifers, clouds of smoke pouring from its chimney and the hearth of fire in front of it.

At the small wooden table in front of the house sat a woman, probably in her mid-twenties, rosy hair, wearing a colourful dress scattered with bright flowers all over, and swinging her feet back and forth as she laughed because of something someone from within the house said to her.

Silene stumbled a step back when someone who painfully re-assembled her younger brother stepped out into the garden, laying two plates of food on the table. He was much older though, his face scarred, his body so much taller, shoulders filled with muscle she could never imagine her brother having from how little they were allowed to eat and how much he was forced to work in the mines.

A bright, teary grin spread on her face when she realised there was nothing left of the man she used to know. That he'd become better, grown, was happier.

She was about to turn and leave, happy with the closure she'd gotten, when the rosy haired woman screeched as he howled her over his shoulder, "Luke! Put me down!"

A sob escaped her, and she spun fast in his direction, losing footing and collapsing to the ground, her eyes filled with too many tears to see her brother clearly no matter how hard she tried to wipe them away. Why had she called him that name?

No. No. No. Luke Carver was gone. Luke was gone. He couldn't be Luke again.

She cried and cried, sobbing onto the hem of her skirt to stop herself from making any sound. What did this mean? Had he been sentenced to a fate like hers?

Az had to know. She had to ask Az.

When she braced a hand on the tree and pushed herself to stand, a branch cracked under her foot and the air went silent. Very slowly, as if afraid she'd startle some wild animal, she looked up at where the commotion had stopped, not expecting two pairs of eyes on her.

He was looking straight at her. Not through her as all humans did. No, her brother, or who had once been her brother, was looking right at her. "Silene?"

She gasped, starting to back away, and dashing in a run through the forest that wilted under her forbidding touch.

"Silene!" Luke shouted, and she ran faster, her sobs bleeding out into the forest. "Silene, I know it is you."

Finally, she stopped even though the boat to Asphodel was only a few feet away. She'd left once like a coward, and though she did not dare ask for his forgiveness, he was owed an apology—for what she'd done to him, the brother she'd loved so dearly, harder than anyone.

"How is this even possible?" he asked, reaching for her, but she backed away, half astound at seeing her brother again and half terrified of what might have happened to him to be forced to remember her. Did he also have nightmares as she did?

Silene pressed a hand to her mouth and cried. No. No. No. She backed away even further. "You can't touch me. I don't even know how you can see me, but...you can't touch me."

Luke's gaze wilted with such pain. "Why not?"

"Nothing I touch can live."

He frowned at her—her little brother frowned at her. Then he smiled. And as he did so, she was struck, transported back in time. That smile was so like the brother she remembered. "You found me. That is all that matters," he said.

"I never looked for you, Luke," she confessed, holding a shaky hand to her heart that felt as though it would fall through her stomach.

Her brother's face fell, as did hers when he said, "I looked for you everywhere, Lena."

The rosy haired girl appeared at his side, clinging to his arm. "You're his."

Luke looked between her and I, confusion marring his eyes.

"You're Azriel's," the woman continued. "That's why your brother could not find you."

"For what I did," Silene started, feeling time slip through her fingers. "Death wanted retribution."

Her brother's expression bled with fury. "I'm going to kill Azriel." Luke put both hands to his brow, shaking his head. "I'm going to kill him, Aurora."

The rosy haired girl, Aurora, gave a look of pity at both of them. "He would not be allowed to tell you, you know that, Luke." She turned to Silene. "As do you, I suppose."

Something struck Silene. "How do you know of him? How do you know Az?"

Luke would not look at her. "Because I am now like him."

"A God," Aurora said. "Vengeance. Gabriel gave him another life. In exchange—"

Silene tensed. "In exchange for what?"

The woman glanced at her brother. "That he would haunt each and every soul with Gabriel's help and slay them for him because he could not."

Silene staggered a step back. "What souls?"

"Of those that hurt you," Luke told her.

He was there when she returned to Asphodel, right across the river—a river that felt like a thousand worlds apart the more seconds passed.

"You now know," he said.

"I do."

"What is your judgement, my ruin? Am I to be spared for what I have done?"

"And what have you done?" she asked, crossing the bridge to his side and kneeling beside him.

He raised a hand to her face, letting his finger ghost down her nose, her eyes, her lips. "Found you too late."

For the first time, Silene longed, burned to be touched. Her insides seared from desire to climb into his lap and bury herself in his chest. She'd finally picked her next grave, and the earth was so gentle to her this time. But somehow, this time...she was afraid. She was so afraid, out of her mind with fear that she would not remember the earth she was buried in.

Silene found the need, the utter desperation to lean into his hands and let him do it, no matter the cost, but to her unfortunate luck, he pulled away.

"I've come to realise that I do not regret the life I had. It is the life my little brother loved me in," Silene admitted. "But I know I will regret the next one. Neither of you will be in it. I will remember neither of you."

"Silene—"

"Please," she begged, and he stood, shaking his head. "You cannot leave me. You still have not given me my last demand."

He chuckled, shaking his head. "Fishing? You're really thinking about fishing at this moment?"

She brought her knees to her chest, swaying there back and forth. "I have no other tricks up my sleeve, Gabriel. How do I fool *time* any other way?"

"You will be happy in your new life, my ruin. You will be so happy, that I can promise you."

How could he not know? How could he not know that she was happy now?

Eleven o' Clock

ONE LAST DEMAND. THAT was all that kept her in his reach. One he was forced to not delay any longer. He couldn't. If any more time passed, he'd do something that might hurt her. He'd hold onto her. He'd refuse to let go of her. And he couldn't hold onto her. He had to let her go.

He knocked on the glass window of her kitchen that framed her like painting in an art gallery, and she spun in his direction. Something akin to an earthquake raked his body when she pressed a hand to the window and gave him something he had not imagined her ever giving him even in his wildest dreams—a smile so radiant she could outshine any sun.

It felt as if something was dragging barbed wire through his insides when he lifted his fingers and pressed them against the cold glass, over hers.

Her little careful smile grew as she watched their hands join, it bloomed into a grin, and for the first time in his existence, he learned what spring felt like to humans.

Leaning closer, she closed her eyes and pressed her lips to the glass.

Tears streaked down his face as he leaned in, too, wishing he could love closely without hurting those he loved.

They stood there, both on each side of the window, their brows pressed together, gazing at one another until her lips moved to form words that sealed so many fates.

It's okay.

Was it though?

Pushing away from the window, she got up and came outside, stopping the closest she'd ever been to him and handing him the end of a ribbon before dragging him to sit on the grass where she'd laid a blanket. "Azriel might throw a fit again if he sees you here."

"He doesn't scare me."

"I envy you," she said, trailing the tip of her finger on the open edge of his leather jacket. "Wish I was afraid of nothing, too."

"I might have lied to you, Silene. There are things that terrify me."

She looked up at him. "What could ever terrify a God like you, Gabriel?"

"Ask me if I have ever been in love."

Silene hesitated, staring up at him with a plea in her eyes for him to take back his words. Her voice was small as she asked, "Have you ever been in love?"

Skies overhead rumbled with thick thunder as he admitted, "I am."

It felt like every clock had stopped moving at that very second, stuck onto those two words as Silene uttered two quiet words of her own, "You are?"

"Yes," he said as the wind picked up and grew into a tempest. Even nature wanted to stop him. "There is this secret I've kept since forever, you see."

She tucked a wind billowed strand of hair behind her ear. "What secret?"

Thunder struck close by. "One night, as I was sitting and staring at the stars, watching wishes being sucked into their bright bellies, I happened to hear one. One made *for* me, but not to me. All of which was strange because who could ever make wishes in my stead," he said with a forlorn smile. "The wish had been for me to vanish, to disappear, to find the worst ends one could ever find, to die a death so deadly I would never wake."

A tear streaked down Silene's cheek as she stared at him aghast.

"Nothing had made me laugh harder," he admitted, staring back at the owner of that wish. "After the amusement wore off, I remember staring at the skies for a long while wondering—wondering what I had done. It nearly gnawed me alive until I stole that prayer from the stars and went to find its owner." He tilted his head towards the stormy skies warning him and threatening him to remain silent as he had remained all these years. Begging him not to tempt fates. "I still have that prayer by the way."

Trees and grass and even the foundations of the hills around them shook from the wind that swept across.

Another tear dropped down her face, and he made to reach for her, his hand halting mid-way the forbidding space between them.

"I found her," he continued, tucking that desire in the place he buried every other desire of his, deep in the chambers of his heart that had grown so big to accommodate his only love—the chambers that had become a graveyard where he'd had to bury his love, too. "A few times actually. I couldn't stop watching her from afar. I kept wondering if such a lovely ghost had been left behind by my brother. I kept wondering why she was still in my lands, amongst my living. Until I saw her tears. Then there she was, my sad girl, alive and all mine yet not mine at all. I could only get so close to her. Even the earth beneath her feet hated me, the walls of her home screamed at me when I'd dare steal any glance, the forest around her home would laugh at my efforts to get her attention. Nothing impressed her. Whenever I'd send her sun, she would go out less. When I'd send her rain, she would curse at it. When I'd grow flowers under her feet, she'd stomp on them. When I'd send her friends, she'd cower in fear. Her being would fade in and out of existence. Sometimes I would not be able to find her for days, nature tricking me and disguising her home. I didn't see her for a long time after. But then she made another prayer for my ruin. I wanted to see her again, but she had to let me somehow."

Silene's lips trembled when she asked. "And did she?"

"She did." A bitter laughter poured out of him. "But it was only to spite me. She was already in my brother's arms when I got

there. She'd hated me so much that it had made her longing for
him almost seem like love—deep, profound love. A love so strong
that she'd drank poison for it. To be close to him."

Another tear slid down Silene's cheek, and Gabriel resisted
every urge that commanded his holy existence to have her in his
arms.

"I begged him," he confessed, finally free of the truth he knew
would make her hate him even more. "I begged him to leave her.
I asked him for a favour. But there isn't much he could take from
me. So I gave him the only thing I could give him—the thing I
would come to desire most. And he left her. The debt for her life
paid in exchange for what I'd come to desire most." He ran a hand
over his eyes, feeling a painful sting burn across them. "I'd made
a mistake in my calculations. I'd underestimated just how much
she hated me and loved him." A choked laughter sputtered out
of him. "The moment we'd left and she'd woken—she'd woken
desperate for her one true love and had bled out in the bed I'd left
her alive on in exchange for the last thing anyone could take from
me. Then I saw her walk through the gates to my brother, right
back in his arms. She'd taken something from him. Twice. He was
not gentle to her. For she then had to serve him for five hundred
years and bring him one hundred thousand lives."

The sob that drew out of her shook his entire being. Unable to
see her crumble right there, so close to him, unable to hold her, he
forced his eyes shut and put his hands over his ears. He couldn't
see or hear her—he could not. He'd hold her, and she'd vanish
in his hands like mist along with any memory he had of hers. He
couldn't—he couldn't live without a fragment of her memory.

Her tears spilled—they'd spilled worse than any blood in any
battle Gabriel had ever witnessed. Then rain fell down on them
with the fury of a thousand storms, bleeding into the land just like
her cries.

And again, all he could do was watch.

Her cries had eventually stopped, but her tears had not. And their silence was most unbearable. Her tears had endlessly poured as he'd helped her dry her hair and change her clothes. They'd not stopped as he'd tried to gently brush her hair and then help her get into her bed.

Laying on her side, facing away from him, she hid them, too. He'd laid beside her with her tucked to his chest as close as he could get, yet somehow it was the furthest he'd ever been to her.

His fingers tangled on the ends of her hair, playing with the strands and marvelling at the softness, remembering how her touch felt the same, so silky and gentle.

"Tonight," she whispered, her voice hoarse and defeated. "Azriel has asked me to collect my last death. What will happen after...with you...and me?"

"You will be reborn."

"And you?"

"I will get to watch you live," he said, smiling, dreaming.

"Will I see you?"

"No, my ruin, to your luck you won't. But I will be there. In the sun, the flame of a candle, city lights, and every single moon beam. I will always be with you."

She sobbed into the pillow. "What if you can't find me again?"

"I'm never losing you again, Silene. I will rake through every world I know to find you. You will not see me, you will not remember me, but I will be there, you have my word. Will you stop sulking and let me look at you now?" Pushing himself up on his elbow, he carefully reached with the back of his finger to push the white strands of hair away from her eyes. "Don't cry, my ruin, my beautiful damnation, or I might not let you go."

"Then don't."

"You deserve better than my wretched heart that can't even love you properly, closely. You deserve someone who can hold you."

She turned and pressed her face to her pillow, her shoulders shaking from the loud sobs.

"Please," he begged, not even able to touch her, to comfort her in his embrace because his words no longer seemed to. "Please, Silene. Please, my ruin."

But she only cried harder.

He did not know how he'd dragged her out of her room, or even out of her home at all and into a very tiny fishing boat in the middle of a lake, holding a fishing rod with both hands and standing stiffly on her seat out of fear they'd topple over and sink in the water.

This had been her last demand.

She wanted to go fishing, but apparently, she had no clue what fishing entailed at all.

"They were smiling with all their teeth and gums in that human magazine," she grumpily muttered, tightening her hold on the fishing rod until her knuckles turned white. "And it stinks in here." She nudged the bait box with the tip of her heeled boots. "Throw that over."

Gabriel shook from laughter, and she squealed when the boat rocked, "Stop laughing, I hate swimming."

He leaned to fold back the brim of the huge fishing hat she'd insisted on wearing and was covering more than half her face. "This is ridiculous."

"I wanted the full experience."

"Did you now?"

After giving him one long look, she sighed and looked away, her shoulders slouching.

"What was all that for?" he asked.

"I want to sit in your lap and kiss you."

He grinned at her. "I want that, too."

"Give me a bargain then, just like you've given the others."

"Silene—"

"Take anything you want, anything at all, just make it so I can have you at least in one lifetime. Any lifetime. Hundreds and thousands of years from now, or at the end of all times, just once, even if it is just for a day. Make it possible. You can do that."

He shook his head. "I can't, Silene."

Her mouth quivered when she looked away at the distance surely to hide her welling eyes while she muttered, "Useless God."

It should have hurt him, but her words only made his heart well. "You can be cruel to me, my ruin. I do not mind."

She sniffled. "You had no business bringing me back then. Wasting a bargain on such a useless thing."

"I was going to give you everything. When you'd wake, I was going to lay the heads of those who hurt you like cobble stone for you to walk on, and with their blood I would have painted a bright red path for you to follow towards a new life, a better one."

Still looking at the distance of the glittering, sun-kissed lake, she muttered, "Something would have been missing."

"What is that?"

Gabriel's heart sank below the very water they stood upon when she turned to look at him. No words were spoken, yet all of them at once. "Perhaps...it happened so—"

"Do not say it," he begged.

Silene looked away again, refusing to show him her face as she whispered, "Stupid, silly God."

His smile only seemed to set her off more because she hurled all sorts of insults at him. All which only made him smile harder.

Twelve o' Clock

SILENE HAD AGED THE rest of her day and all night after collecting her last death, staring out of her window at where Gabriel had stood across the river, sitting by the edge, his head hanging between his knees.

"Look up at me," she whispered as the sunless dawn started rising in her world in lilac hues. "Look up at me, please."

And as if he'd heard her, he did.

"I'm sorry," she whispered, pressing her hand to the window, trailing his faraway silhouette, wishing she could just touch him just once more.

Again, as if he'd heard her, he shook his head, a look of utter defeat falling over his eyes as they left hers again.

"Tell me goodbye," she begged. "At least come and tell me goodbye."

The candle on her vanity burned alive, and she turned to find a letter beside it.

No more than just a sentence was written across it.

My beautiful, beautiful demise, live long and well.

"Coward," she murmured, tears clinging to her eyes. "You coward."

Ink started appearing on the letter, new words forming. *I am.*

"Come here," she whispered.

Not if I am to ever let you go.

She shook her head. "Then don't."

I love you.

Her knees gave to the ground, her body merely a pile of bones surrendered to the grave she'd opened in her own chest.

Silene had done something she thought she'd never do—she'd asked for a bargain.

And Azriel had done the most senseless thing she'd ever seen him do—he'd accepted.

With her new debt in her hand, she made her way towards Asador, almost climbing the stairs to his home two at a time, too impatient and afraid of losing precious minutes to take the lift.

She'd not even waited for her breaths to even out before she'd rasped her knuckles against the door as loud as she could. Even when he'd stood there, eyes red and tear stained, astound at her presence, she had not waited before she'd thrown her arms around his neck and held him as tight as she could.

"Silene," Gabriel breathed in panic, trying to move away from her, but she only held him tighter, tighter than she'd held onto anything before.

"It's okay," she breathed over his skin, smiling when the pain only crippled her heart. "You can't hurt me."

"What?" he shakily asked, putting an unsteady hand at the back of her head and pressing his nose to the crown of her head, inhaling her so deeply as if he was taking his first ever breath. "How...how is this possible?"

"I asked Azriel for a favour," she confessed.

That's when he moved away, pulling back from her as if she

was on fire, panic turning his blue eyes a dark sapphire. And she helplessly, wordlessly watched as he drowned behind them. "My brother grants no favours. What have you done, my ruin? What have you done?" he asked, crumbling to his knees and pressing both of his hands to his face. "What have you done?"

Tears clung to her lashes when she forced a trembling smile on her face and climbed onto his lap. Her happiness turned uncontrollable as she was finally able to do what she'd wished for, despite grief turning her corpse into a catacomb filled with helplessness. "Please," she begged, guiding his weakened and lifeless limbs around her own and burying her face in his chest as she had dreamed of doing so many nights. When his scent of lavender filled her lungs, a strangled cry left her lips.

"Why do you cry, my sad girl?" he said, his fingers still shaking as he touched her face and leaned to kiss her tears away.

"I'm happy."

With a finger under her chin, he tipped her head up and pressed his lips to hers in a crushing kiss. There was no time to brace the impact of that one kiss. Or of the more that were to come.

Silene finally gave away to the sea.

And the sea did not drown her.

After one detailed session on how to properly prepare tea which had included him clinging behind with every step she had taken, after baking him a few cupcakes with her special buttercream which she had made sure to leave behind a detailed recipe for, and after chasing Tommy around and playing with every possible toy of his before nearly cuddling him to death, they'd finally settled quietly on the sofa.

He'd laid her on top of his naked chest as they both mindlessly watched some strange documentary on the television. Neither of them was paying any attention to it. He was entirely too preoccupied tracing his fingers everywhere he could on her body while she was entirely enthralled by the sound of his heart as she pressed her ear to his chest.

"Gabriel?" she asked, smiling when she heard his pulse quicken.

"Yes, my beautiful ruin?"

She pushed herself up onto her hands, caging him between her arms as she stared down at the eyes she could swear changed shades every once in a while. After she was satisfied with her close observations, she poured about a thousand pecks down on his face that had him chuckling like a fool.

His arms banded around her, his hands sneaking under her shirt and settling against her naked back. "There were so many places I wanted to take you," he said, moving his palms up and down her spine. "Let me take you."

"This is the only place I wish to be. Nothing else matters. I'm scared nothing else will ever matter to me."

"I want to make this mean something."

She cupped his face. "It means everything."

He shook his head. "This doesn't feel enough. It isn't enough. I wanted to give you everything. I have everything to give, and it was going to be yours to take. Not like this, my ruin, not like this at all."

"I just want you," she whispered, trailing a finger down the hard panes of his stomach and lower over the deep muscle ridges on his hips that disappeared under his trousers.

"I'm all yours to have," he breathed.

She pulled her hand back when he let out a pained groan. "What's wrong?"

"It feels so good, Silene."

"Oh," she whispered, continuing to trace the lines of his stomach, watching the myriad of expressions cross his face and the way his chest rose faster and faster each time.

He pulled her to his chest, kissing the crown of her head repeatedly and hugging her nearly to suffocation. "Let me make you feel good, too."

"I don't know if I can," she murmured. "It has never felt good before."

"You can, my beautiful ruin," he said, hooking a gentle finger under her scarf and slowly pulling it off, the scalloped edges of the lace material kissing her skin as it slid over it.

He sat up with her on his lap, his strong fingers weaving into the back of her head to grasp her long hair and angle her head back as he pressed his mouth to her scar, licking the length of it and then the column of her throat before he grasped her lips again. "Can I see what's under the tablecloth?"

She could not help but smile against his mouth as he kissed her. "You might want to take Tommy to another room."

"I'd rather have a witness to my murder."

"I'm going to get you very naked, Gabriel."

"I'm pretty certain he's somewhat deaf and partially blind."

Her giggles filled the room, and he grinned up at her, his eyes flashing so many shades of blue.

Pressing his brow to hers, he sighed. "You're perfect. How can you fit so perfectly in my hold yet be the only thing I can't hold onto forever? How can you be made for me so perfectly yet be the one thing I cannot have?" he whispered as he kissed her neck, her shoulder, her arms, her hand, the tips of her finger, anywhere he could.

Reaching for the edges of her shirt, she pulled it up and over her head. The rest of her clothing followed until she stood before him bare and wanting. Even needing—desperately needing him. "You have me."

"Say it again," he demanded, his touch barely a whisper against her skin, like the gentle graze of spring wind, tentative and careful as he trailed the curves of her breasts until her limbs melted against his hold. "Tell me you're mine like I am forever yours."

When his hand came around her throat, wrapping there so gently as if she was a flower stem, her eyes drew shut. "I'm yours."

He drew a nipple in his mouth, rolling his eyes up at her as he licked and sucked and bit her flesh, turning her entire body to liquid. Gabriel took his time with her, his lips and tongue exploring every dent and dip, tasting every inch of her skin until she was panting and on the cusp of begging.

Grasping her jaw with one hand, he kissed her while his other hand cupped and kneaded her breast, his fingers circling the hardened bud. He pulled back only so he could bring two fingers to his mouth to lick them. "I wanted to learn your body," he said, lowering those fingers between her legs and pressing them to the apex of her sex, rubbing slow circles over her sensitive flesh until her legs were buckling and a moan flew out of her lips, only to be swallowed by him. "If only we had more time, I would have taken my time with every dip and curve. Tasted every inch of your skin until it would be branded in my memory until the very end."

"Please," she begged between kisses, as pressure built up down her spine and at her core.

"Don't beg me, my ruin. Order me. Tell me what you need."

"You."

He smiled over her lips as her fingers slid down her sex, teasing her wet entrance. "I need you to be a little more precise. A finger?" he asked, pushing one inside her and leaving her gasping. "Or two?" He nipped at her lips as a second one filled her, pushing them in and out of her until her limbs began trembling. "Or my cock? Fuck, you're so wet. Maybe you want my cock. Tell me and I will give you anything you want."

"Enough playing," she breathed, her chest rising and falling fast. "Just have me."

Sliding his fingers out of her, he brought them to his mouth, licking the both of them clean. "As you wish," he said, lifting her up just enough to reach and remove his trousers. The man or God before her looked drunken, in an utter haze as he pressed his lips all over her before reaching between them with a hand and angling her hips with the other.

She gasped in his mouth when she felt the thick head of his cock nudge at her sex. But he did not push in just yet, he waited until she softened in his arms again, smearing her wetness over the length of her sex and teasing that centre of nerves at the apex of her thighs that had her gasping for new air—air that only he could breathe back in her lungs. He didn't have to push in at all because Silene lowered herself on him, making them both groan. She sank down his cock bit by bit, moaning as she stretched her insides. "God," she breathed, her eyes screwed shut.

One of his hands came to the back of her neck, wrapping to hold her there as he kissed her. "I'm right here."

"Arrogant prick."

"That is inside you," he cooed, his hips bucking up to remind her of just that, and he slid even deeper inside her.

Bracing her hands on his shoulders, she slowly rocked on his thick length, feeling her core heat up with each sway.

"My Silene," he breathed in her mouth as his hands came down the curves of her body and settled on her hips while she slowly rode him. "My beautiful Silene."

Her eyes drew shut as pressure built in her core. "I...I can't."

Hooking his hands under her knees, he lifted the both of them up and laid her down on the sofa, on her back, hovering over her and taking the opportunity to suck on both her breasts before he grabbed his cock with one hand and pushed it in her again. "Open your legs wider for me, Silene," he said, bracing both his hands on either side of her, and she felt her cheeks heat up. "That's it, my beautiful ruin, let me see."

She was sure she'd gone entirely red under his perusal.

Her legs wrapped around his thighs, and she watched where they joined, running her hands down his chest as he thrust in her gently, slowly. Then their eyes locked, the world disappearing as he made love to her, as he brought her near an edge nothing had ever brought her before. One that had her vision filled with stars and her lungs drowning with air. An edge he'd followed her to.

Spent and breathless, he pulled her on top of his naked body, his mouth pressing to the top of her head in a dozen kisses.

She'd never made love like that. Silene had never really made love at all. She hated the way bile rose to her throat at the memories of how her innocence had been ripped away. How she'd been merely an object on the other hands that had held her. "I wish this had been my first. I wish you'd been my first."

His hold on her grew tighter. "I am your first."

"But—"

He trailed the back of his hand down her cheek so gently despite the look of such utter fury painted in his face. "Your brother killed them all, and I burned every single soul who took what you did not give permission to take. They no longer exist. I burned their pasts and their futures, every trace of their existence. The only place they haunt is here," he said, pressing a finger to her brow, "and soon they will be gone forever."

"There are other things that haunt me there," she admitted. "I like how he haunts me."

The skies in his eyes turned glassy. "Then I shall haunt you, my great ruin."

Tipping her head up, she pressed her mouth to his. "I will be waiting for it. Should we wash up?"

"I was planning on dirtying you up again."

Just then, her stomach did something it had not done in centuries—it growled with hunger, making him drop his head back and laugh.

"Food it is," he said, grabbing his shirt and throwing it over her head, guiding her arms through the short sleeves before sitting her up in his lap and wrapping her legs around his waist. With her clinging to him like that, he started making her food.

Then he'd made love to her again right there in his kitchen, then as he'd brought her under the hot shower, and again in his bed until their limbs were tangled together to the point neither knew where the other started and where they ended.

"If I gave you a dream, any dream, what would you want to dream about?" he murmured, his eyes fluttering from sleep. "I will give it to you."

"Too late," she whispered. "I got my dream."

They'd fought sleep hard, the both of them.

But exhaust and grief had meddled in a strange concoction and drowsed them.

Time had done the most unforgivable thing.

It had passed.

As she stared down at his sleeping form sprawled on the bed, she started counting down the seconds that would soon strike to dawn, trying not to let the last memory of him blur behind tears.

"I will remember," she whispered to herself as she choked on chopped sobs. "How can I forget? I can't forget. Nothing could make me forget you."

Seconds before her own clock would finally strike a second death, she reached a hand to his face, forcing herself to remember every detail on his skin, the exact way he felt at her touch, the colour of his hair that she hoped to forever see in the sun.

She pressed her lips to his brow as gently as she could without waking him up in the new cold world of hers. "You are so beautiful. You are so beautiful to me."

Holding her *timekeeper* tightly to her chest, she wished one last time that it would stop working. And when more seconds were wasted away on wishes that couldn't be fulfilled, she gathered every little bit of strength she had to stand and leave and not scream: *Let me be just a ghost only to haunt you for I can no longer love you.*

Her heart could never be hollow or narrow enough not to fit him. It was a but a wretched thing, blackened by misery and bruised by hopelessness, but she would behold him like a beacon.

Azriel was waiting for her right against the gates to his world, his head lowered in a defeat that *Death* never accepted. There was no hopelessness in death, so why were his endless, dark eyes drowning in it? "I am sorry," he whispered, low and dark and mournful.

It was then Silene let it all out. Everything she had held in.

She crumbled in the only arms she could ever allow herself to crumble, she'd crumbled in his arms one too many times, and he'd welcomed it every single time.

"I don't want to forget him."

He would not look at her, his hopeless gaze latching on her palms pressed against each other at her chest, her only shield against the pounding of her heart begging to be set free. "You both made unbreakable bargains, Silene. There are worse things than forgetting," he said. "Remembering is one of them."

"What will I remember?" she asked, hopeful despite all the signs of dread already marking her.

"Of him? Nothing. You will never remember him for long even if you meet again. You will start anew in my service. For five hundred more years."

Time passed, it was what it did best, but she didn't want it to make her forget. "And then?"

He shook his head. "Only the *Fates* know." A flicker of something less than hope and more than despair glistened in his eyes. "Maybe they will be kind."

Despite all the strength she used to hold her tears back, she broke again. "They never are."

Epilogue

GABRIEL HAD BEEN BESTOWED with a curse. The curse of memories. Memories he shared with no one now. Memories he'd once shared with someone he loved. Someone he'd always love. Someone who'd never even remember ever loving him back again.

He'd watched his dead lover for hundreds of years now as he'd always done. Sometimes from afar, and at other times when he'd mustered the courage to bear the brunt force of longing, he could do it from up close.

This spring morning, she had watched him back. They'd sat merely a few feet apart on opposite benches on the small park she often visited every spring in Asador as they had once done long ago together, in a faraway memory she could not remember and one he would never forget. When his gaze had finally become unbearably noticeable, she'd lowered the book she'd been reading and simply stared at him. Seconds had turned into minutes. Minutes into hours. He could see the tumultuous storms brewing in her gaze, the many questions she had but unable to recall the answers she'd once had for all of them.

He could swear flashes of pain marred the colour of her irises; a haze of tears had glazed them from frustration.

Her lips parted and she made to speak words she simply couldn't recall. Her teeth dug on the corner of her trembling mouth as she struggled with the words, "I know you, don't I?"

His heart painfully pounded against his ribs, begging to be let out, begging to be handed back onto her gentle hold. "You do."

She swallowed, a tear escaping from her eye, and she sucked in a shaky breath, her lip quivering. "Who are you?"

And he'd introduced himself to her again, he'd told her their story, for the hundred or thousands of times. On a spring morning like many spring mornings before over the years. And like every other time, when day would fade, when light would start to disappear into midnight, she'd forget him. And once again, he'd be a stranger to her, and she'd be the creation he'd beheld with such violent hands.

Tales would follow for years, and they would tell their story with a different path each time, but always the same ending. That Gabriel had loved the ghost of a woman Silene had been after her bargain with Death for endless years, and that she had never loved him back for longer than a day.

Despite it, no one would speak of what the fates had decided for them at the end of her second curse. They only knew that life had gone on, and that he'd never quite forgiven himself for that.

...

But some also say that the Reaper fell in love one last time after her five hundred years of her service ended. Whispers would say that it was the last love for the God of Life, too. One he'd waited for so long, one he never let go of.

And that their love was eternalised.

That she never would leave his side again.

That their love also bore fruit.

A child so loved by the both of them.

Nor human, nor God.

An omen so dear, so pure and gentle that humanity loved her, too. One that grew bright in the darkest moments. Something akin to hope and light.

And such some would say.
But tales are kind. So kind.
And *Fates* were not.

The end.

Afterword

This might be turning into a dear diary moment, but I like yapping and you are reading this book which means you've automatically entered an agreement to hear me yap.

You have no idea how many times I've rewritten this book. I can say that I did love this story almost to its death because I literally have reworked this story so, so many times.

Ultimately, it might have been a mistake, or it might have not been, but it is what it is, and this was the last time I put a single word on this book, I had to let it go or I was going to just bury it somewhere.

Really hope it isn't a disappointment, because this one is the nearest and dearest to my heart out of all the three I've published so far.

Acknowledgements

I want to thank so, so many of you, but this time round I want to thank everyone who has picked up and read these novellas. It absolutely blows my mind that so many people have read them. I swear these were just going to be some stress relief side projects for me as they were already resting on my editor's desk with my other million works in progress. To anyone who had no idea what these books were and still gave them a go, thank you so, so much!

I want to thank Jada, miss Jada Ronan for literally being the backbone of my mental health these past few weeks.

I want to thank a few of my readers, Oana, Anastasia, Chaitanya, Jazlyn, Meg, Nicole, Ruby, who have been my cheerleaders on the *Wult* (my little reading group).

And lastly, I want to thank my sister for staying alive. Hope you do that for a long time, you little bi—

About the author

Wendy Heiss is a indie author debuting with a new adult fantasy trilogy, Winter Gods & Serpents, the first book in The Auran Chronicles. She has graduated with a Forensics Science degree in the United Kingdom, but literature has been one of her passions since she could manage to read and write. Despite being severely tempted to ride the Agatha Christie route to crime novels, she chose to follow the Tolkien path to fantasy. She forwent fingerprint powder for ball pen ink inevitably forgoing her parents hope for a good life and becoming what they always feared...a figuratively starving artist, which is why she won't quit her day time job any time soon.

Any whom and how, she likes cats, coffee, particularly that cr*p from instant sachets. Loves, loves when spring doesn't try to give her at least one asthma attack every year and threaten her life. 'Claims' to despise mafia romance from the pits of her gall bladder but will probably end up writing one herself to try and outwrite the greatest line in history: Are you alright, babygirl?

Also, fried sweet potatoes, she can definitely eat some of those without claiming to be allergic to yet another vegetable. On that last note before straying too far from a simple bio, please read her books.

Also by

Printed in Dunstable, United Kingdom